Under the Shadow

Gilbert Sorrentino

Dalkey Archive Press

Library of Congress Cataloging-in-Publication Data
Sorrentino, Gilbert.
  Under the shadow / Gilbert Sorrentino. — 1st ed.
  I. Title.
PS3569.O7U54   1991   813'.54—dc20   91-15014
ISBN: 0-916583-84-8

First edition

Some sections of this work have appeared in *Conjunctions*, to whose editor
the author makes grateful acknowledgment.

Partially funded by grants from The National Endowment for the Arts and
The Illinois Arts Council.

Dalkey Archive Press
1817 North 79th Avenue
Elmwood Park, IL 60635 USA

*Printed on permanent/durable acid-free paper and bound in the United States
of America.*

Wherefore are these things hid? Wherefore have these gifts a
curtain before 'em?

—*Twelfth Night*, I, iii

❧ CONTENTS ❧

Under the Shadow

⧽ MEMORIAL ⧼

The friends and business acquaintances of the dead man, gathered in a perfectly appointed town house for a hastily arranged memorial service, are dressed as if for a costume party. The deceased's fiancée, the casual focus of curious eyes, is clad as a Crusader who feigns—such is the excellent masquerade—womanhood. At the moment, she is making a gesture of rejection to a man kneeling before her in shapeless white robes, his arms spread in supplication, adoration, or complaisance. The red cross on the woman's fleur-de-lis-spangled gypon catches glancingly the candlelight which illuminates the lavishly furnished buffet. Beyond, in slightly menacing shadows, her ancients and advisors hover. One might think that the kneeling man is in some actual danger, but this is not the case.

The deceased, so fragments of conversation and gossip gathered here and there suggest, apparently swallowed a bottle of poison at the table of an undistinguished restaurant known for its heavy sauces, too rich desserts, and haphazardly placed bowls of unidentifiable spheroids, many of them translucent.

There is the sweet chiming of a teaspoon against a crystal wineglass. The guests break off their conversations, refresh their drinks, and form a loose cluster at one end of the drawing room, at the other end of which, the deceased's fiancée, looking now quite genuinely masculine, holds up a small painting. It depicts a kitchen window seen from just beyond a wooden fence. Behind the streaked, dirty pane, the blurred figure of a scowling young woman can be descried. She seems to be naked, or partially naked, and with her left hand stiffly held before her, makes a gesture of rejection. The fiancée, whose name is Jeanne Sousa, or Souze, holds the painting higher, and speaks. "Friends," she begins, her voice low with emotion, or, perhaps, feigned emotion.

≫ FIRE ≪

The publisher, Emiliano Soreau, has recently become enthralled by old news accounts of what was sensationally called "the holocaust of books," "the maniac's inferno," and, less often, "the destruction of evidence." He confides to close friends in the communications-and-media industry, or, as cynics sometimes describe it, the publishing business, that he'd very much like to find a top-notch professional writer—perhaps a cultural journalist turned powerhouse novelist—to do a history of the fire. He'd like someone with flair and intelligence and a respect for the public's well-defined taste, someone to evoke the day itself, the events leading up to the disaster, the people and accidents and coincidences, as well as, of course, as Mr. Soreau puts it, "the blunders and heartaches, the heroism and cowardice, the self-sacrifice of so many plain, ordinary people, the laughter, the tears, the joy and the agony, the searing questions and shocking answers, the sober postmortems, the *why*." His colleagues nod and smile at the sound of these familiar, comforting words. Once again, they realize what a wondrous business they serve.

So far as Mr. Soreau can ascertain, the fire was set by the admitted maniac, Jonathan Tancred, so that he might destroy the entire inventory of the largest book warehouse in the world. According to Tancred, he felt that he was destroying evidence, destroying what he obsessively and repeatedly called "official memories." A transcript of his interrogation notes that he said that "there are too many memories already." In the course of this interrogation, Tancred spoke over and over again of a blue metal laundry hamper, a half-opaque-glass bathroom door which would not close completely, a toy zeppelin, and three young women in luminous white dresses by the shore of a dark lake. He insisted that the razing of the warehouse would allow a new past to be born, a wholly different past.

A photograph taken at the very height of the fire shows a group of firemen fruitlessly battling the terrific blaze. The walls are about to collapse, burying most of them beneath tons of scorching debris. Two of the men, standing on ladders leaning against one of the walls, are surely aware of their imminent doom. In the foreground of the picture, back to the camera, another fireman has a silver bugle slung across his shoulder.

Records reveal that Tancred, when shown this photograph, said that the tunes locked inside the bugle were also official memories, and so he had seen to the disappearance of the horn that very day. As Mr. Soreau reads this, he smiles as the words *Day of the Silver Bugle* come to him. It is wonderful to publish books that one loves, important books, responsible books, books that make a difference! So he thinks.

A week later, Tancred receives a letter from the Soreau Communications Group (SoreCo) at the Pelepzin Hospital for the Criminally Insane. He knows that envelopes contain memories disguised as scripted messages couched in clever alphabetical codes. He tears the letter into strips and, somehow, sets it afire.

⇒ SNOWMAN ⇐

One morning a snowman appeared by the side of the road in front of the country house owned, for many years, by the famous dancer Olga Chervonen. The stark tree behind and to the left of the figure held its usual complement of snow, most of it, not unnaturally, on the windward side of the trunk. Somewhat surprisingly, the snow looked very much like fresh white paint, or, even more surprisingly, like a drawing of fresh white paint, that is, a drawing of, so to speak, nothing. The snowman's face was somewhat debauched, sinister even, although no one remarked on this. No smoke came from Madame Chervonen's chimney, although, inside the house were, in addition to the dancer, Edward Carmichael, the *bel canto* singer; Louis Bill, a charmingly unworldly tool-and-die maker; Isidor Martin, the biologist; and Claude Urbane, the internationally acclaimed polo player. They seemed warm and comfortable as they chatted amiably before a crackling fire. So the lack of smoke was, indeed, perplexing, and remains so.

The snowman, his tiny eyes glittering in the sunlight that slanted through the dead trees, was discovered to be holding a dried branch, which leaned against his shoulder and arm. It may well have been thought of as a rifle or a fishing rod or any number of other things. A staff, for instance. Or a spear. On closer inspection, the snowman's aspect seemed not so much sinister as demented: the fact that his mouth was fashioned from dried leaves, grit, pebbles, and nameless detritus added to this impression. At certain moments, his eyes closed and then opened again, although this probably did not actually happen.

Inside the house, the group of friends talked over the mysterious letter which concerned certain scattered events of some fifty years earlier. The letter spoke of a woman at a sink, a barren backyard, an empty kitchen, and a voice from behind a door. Other occurrences were also detailed, although Louis Bill was hesitant to speak of them, as, indeed, were the others. There was a rumor at the time that a snowfall was also mentioned in the letter. Mentioned in passing, yet mentioned nonetheless. Isidor Martin noticed the snowman, and everyone crowded to the windows. There he was!

⇒ DUSK ⇐

Donald Chainville, a gifted, although inflexibly conservative architect, sits at his study table, leafing through yet another book. He is searching for a passage but dimly remembered, a slightly blurred and hypnotic passage filled with silence. In it, a tall man slowly emerges from a car. He wears a double-breasted navy blue melton overcoat and a grey snap-brim fedora; his face, perhaps innocently, is in shadows. Behind him the pale reds and savage oranges of a bitter-cold winter sunset spread thinly across the sky over Jersey.

There is something ambiguous about the passage, something deliberately closed and dreamlike, and the man, so Chainville seems to recall, is seen through a boy's eyes. As he thinks the word "tall," he stops, momentarily, but realizes, almost instantly, that this word is part of a passage having to do with what he recalls is a sentinel patrolling before an isolated house.

Chainville makes a not uncommon movement of the intelligence, an infinitesimal shifting of reality, so that he becomes the boy in the sought-for passage, the events of the passage become the events of his own past, and the man who steps from the Packard sedan, splendid and terrifying, may be able to answer Chainville's questions, whatever, after all these years, they may be. In the story, the boy runs from the man, in panic, toward home, such as it was. He has no questions for the man, who stands, his hand on the car's open door, one foot on the running board, looking after the boy, who runs and runs.

Chainville's questions? They are centered on fragments of memory, half-memory, smudged images. A tunnel through the snow from a car to a front door, a woman, half-clothed, at a sink, although this image may also be from the book whose passage he seeks, and the woman, or so he remembers, is described therein as a wife, or was she a whore or a young mother? Other questions occur to Chainville as he pulls another book toward him from a small stack on his table, questions about the imagined gaspings of slowly dying love, dim kitchens, reverberant silences, a stony, barren backyard, a boy's terrified weeping.

Chainville is certain that he will not find the passage and he is now equally certain that he doesn't possess a copy of the book. The words of the passage unreel in his mind in a wholly different, one might say new pattern from that which places the man in the street in the icy dusk. They are, now, or so Chainville thinks he knows, the words which the man would have spoken to the boy had the latter not so foolishly run away. They tell of, first, a half-clothed woman in kitchen shadows, who turns to smile. Chainville looks away so as not to stare at her.

⊗ CLUES ⊗

It was on that street, familiar to all, that the adventures took place, although "adventures" is a word not used until much later to characterize the events of the time. No one has admitted to a detailed knowledge of these events, and some, perhaps predictably, argue rather heatedly that there *were* no events. It was, certainly, revealed that Ann Jenn, of the Jenntille Foundations fortune, was at least partially involved, along with Jed Whag, the Clown of Clowns, and Russell Cuiper, known in his day as the inventor of the transverse flute.

Despite all, there were, even then, indications that the street was the focus of what soon developed into a full-blown scandal. Architectural psychologists, however, pointed out that old cobblestones, old shutters, old window boxes, old stoops, and old gas lamps—the last maintained at considerable expense by a bemused tenants' association—while desirable, and even *advantaged,* have neither the structural nor aesthetic power to cause the series of events to which everyone is now quite embarrassedly sensitized. There were a number of clues unearthed, over a period of months, from the puzzling debris discovered in the most unlikely places; money had been, apparently, no object to the pursuit of degradation. Those clues which the authorities have dared make public are: an opaque glass Clasp; a rusted hub Shard; a metal brassiere Cap; a blue enamel Bulb; a Worcestershire sauce Chip; a burnt-out bottle Lace; a nine-inch white Pebble; a frayed cotton Top; and a small shoe Thread. Although the uses to which these items were put, and the scenes of which they speak, have been the subject of horrified speculation both popular and scientific, none of the principals has ever shed light on their meaning. Miss Jenn has long been sequestered by her family in private apartments within the walls of a European convent; Whag no longer speaks, has forgotten how to juggle, and lives amid certain dense fogs; and Cuiper has lost all interest in music, and, instead, gives himself over to a study of Virginia Woolf's handwriting and its relationship to the coif motif in her novels.

For the last few years, investigators have been convinced that Robert Bedu, a genius of applied electronics technology, might, possibly, once have had the answers. Bedu himself hinted at such a possibility on numerous occasions, some festive, others semi-morose. Before he could publish or otherwise broadcast his theories on the relationship of the odd clues to the bizarre and even repulsive incidents, he became obsessed with a dangerous dream technique, variously known as picturebearing, sounddrawing, and fleshtouching. All of the early practitioners of this technique have either died or lapsed into an irreversible catatonic state. At last report, Mr. Bedu was laboring over a letter which will, he asserts, free him from doubt and fear. "Observe my fountain pen," he has been quoted as saying, "isn't it a beauty?" Then it is back to his letter. He seems to have lost all interest in the old scandal.

One rather singular piece of information: for each of the clues in and of itself, and for all of them in combination with certain, or all, of the others, there is always to be discovered a person who, aghast, reads in them the hidden secrets of his or her own life. In some inexplicable way, the clues point everywhere at once.

⇒ HOUSE ⇐

At that place is a slatted-paneled moveable cover on one surface, forming the border of an opening in the wall of the building, for the admission of light and air. It is usually closed by casements or sashes containing transparent materials, in this case, glass, and is capable of being opened and shut.

The open case made for admitting, enclosing, or supporting things is covered with a mixture of pigment and some suitable liquid to form a solid adherent covering when spread on a surface in thin coats (for decoration, protection, etc.). It is of the color of pure snow, reflecting to the eye all the rays of the spectrum combined, as are the slatted-paneled moveable covers.

The structure for human habitation, into one of whose upright enclosing parts this opening in the wall is put into a desired position, is clearly not a recently made one.

It is in the rural regions; or the outlying parts of a city; the structure may, perhaps, be in *any* important town.

The structure is whitened with a composition of lime and water; or whiting, size, and water; or the like.

At that place of low elevation is a concreted-earthy or mineral matter, or a very hard, natural, igneous-rock formation of visibly crystalline texture consisting essentially of quartz and orthoclase (or microline) solid fence, extending side by side with the structure; between it and the structure is an irregularly spread-out—affecting, in some degree, pity or sorrow—woody perennial plant having a single main axis exceeding ten feet in height.

It might be a tree of two closely related genera with pyramidal panicles of small, crimson, one-seeded drupes, and, in one genus, smooth fruits and foliage poisonous to the touch. Or a small Asiatic genus of chiefly tropical trees and shrubs typifying a family having bitter bark, mainly pinnate leaves, and

16 |

small, three-to-five merous flowers. Or a genus of Old World flowering shrubs of the apple family.

Passing downward freely at less than usual speed, and at the identical measure of the amount of turning necessary to bring one line or plane into coincidence with, or parallel to another, are eight lateral outgrowths of a stem of a plant, withered, and of a not-varying or variable red-yellow—of low saturation and low brilliance—in hue.

They are from a different, distinct, or partly or totally unlike woody perennial plant having a single main axis commonly exceeding ten feet in height: one which does not either spring up or mature on this piece of real estate.

At the other side of the opening in the wall, three female persons clothe themselves for the Eucharistic rite of the Latin church.

Their titles, by which any person or thing is known or designated, are not recognized as distinct; their parts of existence, extending from the beginning to any given time, are also not recognized as distinct; their traits, properties, or qualities pertaining to the body: these, too, are not recognized as distinct.

Two of them are in ladies' gowns of the color of pure snow, and the other is in the act of proceeding to cause to slide on easily her lady's gown, in such a way as to cover a one-piece garment of the color of pure snow.

One of the female persons turns the eyes, as if for viewing, out an opening in the wall, and comments on the particular excellence of the partly destitute-of-light, considerable inland body of standing water, which they have, on every occasion, conceived of as theirs.

The fact of this considerable inland body of standing water being so, ascertains by argument (or other evidence) that the structure for human habitation is, in truth, in the rural regions.

Under the present circumstances, the female persons are prepared for some act or event, and withdraw from the space enclosed by a partition. Small pieces of cloth—for wiping the face, nose, or eyes—of delicate, openwork fabric and fine threads of the color of pure snow are fastened with pins so as to envelop their hair.

Each female person holds in the hand a book containing that which is said or sung at Mass for each and every day of the year.

The moveable barrier (usually turning on hinges), by which an entryway is closed and opened, shuts. There is an unforeseen, piercing *absence of sound.*

Eight lateral outgrowths of a stem of a plant pass downward at less than usual speed, all at the identical measure of turning necessary to bring one line or plane into coincidence with, or parallel to another.

One of the slatted-paneled moveable covers collides, with a loud, resounding noise, with the structure for human habitation, in the decidedly below-normal temperature, barely moving air.

⮞ POSTCARD ⮜

The picture postcard depicts an androgynous figure, richly caparisoned in heavy white moire over dazzling armor, sans helmet, astride a sturdy war-horse in the act of bowing his mighty head. The rider holds, vertically, a staff, the butt end of which rests in the right-hand stirrup. From the staff flutters a white banner, that, upon close inspection, seems to be a lace-hemmed slip. Massed behind the young man—or woman—are foot soldiers, armed with spears whose blades are much like long, slender adzes. The figure on horseback is apparently about to lead the men into battle, although it is possible that they are not men, but women. The drawing, design, and colors of the card are of the most inferior quality.

This is, perhaps, the picture postcard—now rather notorious —which was, given the fragile evidence of gossip, bought by Yolanda Philippo, or Emilia Sladky, or Isabella Alcott. The arguments pro and con these women as purchasers of the card are many, and fill three tall file cabinets in the offices of the chemist and trivia collector, Joshua Bex. The very thought of the unsorted documents aggravated, without fail, Bex's incipient duodenal ulcer, and he would, at such times, begin another abstruse experiment with the colored gels on which he had labored for thousands of hours. "Fortuna favet fortibus," he would reply to insolent visitors.

Here is the message on the postcard, which, just as one might guess, is not addressed to anyone.

Despite the near-wintry sunsets and the dismal backyards, the boringly respectable conversations and the yearned-for adulteries, and the usual ups, downs, and arounds of a petty and suffocating academic milieu— cheese and crackers, opera talk, discovered vintages, cigarette hysteria, traffic concerns—there yet are amorous possibilities neither admissible nor imaginable in, perhaps, the spotless kitchen.

Each of the three women had, at one time or another, burgeoning emotional problems; there was, and often, reckless talk of "clanging" steel doors; and, too, the spectacle persisted, of girls, modest yet desirable, with small white handkerchiefs pinned to their hair. Many attributed these phenomena to religion, and that settled the question for them, at least. Yet while documents continued to accumulate, none of them even began to address the most basic questions, i.e.:

who wrote the postcard?

who sent the postcard?

was the postcard ever, indeed, sent?

if sent, who received it?

All this happened years before Joshua Bex took Emilia Sladky as his second wife, at just about the time of the revelations concerning Yolanda Philippo's involvement in the Zeppelin Gallery scandal. Isabella Alcott's rather suspicious death occurred, of course, just weeks after the initial discovery of the postcard. So much for chronology.

Contemporary developments in post-negativity theory suggest that although the *message* of the postcard is essentially illocutionary and, hence, incapable of discourse, the *image* is wholly—and radically—performative. When this idea was suggested to Bex, he immediately set fire to several almost-completed experiments and hid his wife's Indian clubs.

⇒ TREE ⇐

Bill Juillard, a self-taught historian possessed of that which he thought of as total objectivity, came across the true reason for the large tree. For a time, he kept the discovery to himself. No one knew why Juillard, usually quite gregarious and talkative, would do this. The townspeople grew sullen.

Sleep came hard to Juillard. He was not used to carrying such a burden of secrecy.

He noted, although, ultimately, it did not matter, that the tree was an old one; that it could be considered historical; that generations had revered it, more or less, although there had always been an embarrassing minority intent upon drunken holiday fun and furtive adultery, usually committed in parked cars or locked bathrooms, and complete with stains and lost items of clothing.

Juillard tried to describe the tree but there didn't seem to be any point to it, especially since a traveling waiter, passing through on his way to what he called the Annual Feast, told him that the tree looked very much like a mammoth ivy. The waiter, who had been drinking gin for four or five days, may have been mistaken.

Juillard drew a sketch of the tree, which has been preserved, and which was to have accompanied this brief account. It does not appear, for although it is surely a representation of something, that something is not a tree.

The tree reminded Juillard of a sweet and vivacious girl with whom he had been in love when he was nineteen. There seemed no connection between the tree and the girl, but Juillard was inhabited by the tree, and so everything followed the path of the tree.

⋙ POET ⋘

Leonard Bacon, whose legend grows the greater the longer his poems elude discovery, has been dead for twenty-five years, and on the occasion of this anniversary of his demise, his admirers, whose fervor more than makes up for their relatively small number, once again sift through the few facts, the odds and ends of memorabilia, the fleeting references—which, it is to be admitted, multiply with each passing year—that constitute all that is presently known of his fabled life. There is, predictably, a crazed fringe element that insists that Bacon is still alive and that a farmyard animal or large shrub was cremated in his stead. None of the subscribers to this and other demented theories can offer a shred of evidence for their conjectures.

There were few things in Bacon's study able to shed light on the sort of life he led. His address book, although crammed with entries, turned out to be a directory to the dead, the missing, the pseudonymous, and the nonexistent. He had neither parents nor siblings, and was a childless bachelor, whose sexual life was apparently fulfilled in the affectless world of prostitution. His childhood, adolescence, young manhood—in a word, his past— had quite simply vanished as completely as his poetry. In addition to the useless address book, there was left the notorious box of glass phials, a collection of photographs of erotically posed women in, as they say, scanty costume, all of them resembling—astonishingly so!—the First Ladies of the past fifty years, and a copy of *Pirandello—True, or What?*, by Benno DeLux, described as a professor of radical-projection theatre, inscribed "To Leony—with a lot of real awe, Benny." There was also found, of course, the only known photograph of Bacon, a famous image, reproduced so many thousands of times that it has, by now, the familiar presence of a religious icon.

His decision to destroy his voluminous notebooks and manuscripts in a surge of disgust followed a solitary hiking trip through the foothills of the Zo Mountains, so biographical zealots believe. The classic photograph mentioned shows him standing at the edge of a cliff, his feet firmly set, left hand held out for balance, right hand grasping his staff, the latter planted on the ground. Behind him recede vistas of snowy peaks, stretching to the horizon and the pale colors of a wintry sunset. He is wearing trousers—actually, roomy breeches—of bingo cloth, a plait-Mersey sweater with all natural grasses intact, and a Vixit scarf, signed. His staff is a hand-rubbed rumpelstick, whose intricate carvings show depraved scenes of village life, and on his back he carries a small knapsack known to outdoorsmen as a puta bag. His cap, socks, and boots are well-made and sturdy.

He is staring into the distance, astonished that he can see, with perfect clarity, for miles. Far off, there is a half-clothed woman wandering about the barren backyard of a small, one-family brick house. She seems to be searching for someone, or perhaps avoiding someone who is searching for her. She walks aimlessly around the small enclosure, her arms crossed over her icy breasts, her bare thighs blue with cold, her teeth chattering. Bacon takes this sight as revelatory of a profound mystery, the illumination of which will permit him access to the most sublime reaches and truths of art. In understanding this, he instantly realizes the weakness, empty professionalism, and vile transparency of his life's work.

There are—there could not help but be—many questions concerning the photograph: where was it really taken? is that truly snow on the peaks, or light reflected off vast fields of paper? why is Bacon's puta bag so obviously empty? how do we even know that this man *is* Leonard Bacon? and what evidence is there that the poet saw a woman? Each question occasions yet another, each answer demands elaboration. Throughout these lucubrations, Bacon's genius is reaffirmed, strengthened, and marveled at. The thought of what his poems *must have been like* renders his devotees stupid with pleasure.

There is, so far, one line of his verse to have surfaced and to be judged authentic; it is believed to be the last line of a sestina called "Elliptic Derangements":

And yet, what magic in the White Balloon!

It must be confessed that the generally accepted interpretation of the photograph has, of late, come under increasingly heavy attack, especially by—it should come as no surprise—the members of the Balloon League.

☙ MOON ❧

Dr. Ronald LeFlave adjusts the viewfinder on his telescope and prepares to examine the surface of the moon, high and full and gleaming, far above the predictable and complacent town in which he lives alone and practices medicine. He is a mediocre physician, and although he has never been directly responsible for anyone's death, he has made his small contribution to the misery of the world. He has no gift for the medical arts, and to escape the unsatisfying life chosen for him thirty years earlier, he has become something of an astronomer, and at the present time is writing a monograph on aspects of the moon as they relate to mood shifts in the middle-aged professional, in this case, perhaps not surprisingly, himself. He is flattered to find that he has moods, and that they shift, since his mother taught him that moods do not exist.

He peers into the viewfinder, sharpens the focus, and is surprised—amazed would be a better word—to see a man of about thirty-five, splendid in a white linen suit and Borsalino, sitting with three young women in pale pastel dresses and wide straw hats. They are—Dr. LeFlave looks carefully—picnicking in the deep shade of huge trees overhanging the shore of a quiet lake. Dr. LeFlave leans back, alarmed, since the telescope is aimed directly at the moon. He puts his eye to the viewfinder once again.

Although only a few seconds have passed, the man, his hat still on, has mounted one of the young women and their bodies writhe determinedly amid a cloud of white underclothes. The other two young women, some twenty or thirty yards down the shore, have neatly placed their shoes and stockings on the grassy bank, and, their skirts held modestly close to their dainty thighs, wade in the clear shallows. Dr. LeFlave looks back at the lovers, and then, although ashamed, watches, immobile, as they climb into orgasm. One of the young woman's satin slippers dangles tremblingly from the foot which she has convulsively thrust straight up into the mild summer air.

The doctor abruptly pulls himself away from the telescope and the unlikely scene it has somehow discovered. He is aroused, and feels himself on the brink of what Roberto Arlt calls the "blazing darkness" of carnal anguish. How alone he is. Absolutely, profoundly alone, and far from the empty white moon.

⊰ HORN ⊱

The silver fireman's bugle that disappeared on the terrible occasion of the holocaust of books seemingly turned up—its shape radically changed—as a hunting horn, or so Edward Carmichael, the workaday tenor, insisted. He has, still, the horn, or what might be the horn, to prove it, and will produce it from its rather carefully assigned place at the bottom of his cravat drawer on any pretext.

Carmichael is vague as to how the horn found its way into his exclusive possession, but the story concerning his discovery of it is strange enough. On a hunting weekend at the Beckets Ford Hills estate of Sir Evelyn Jenn, Carmichael attests that when the master of the hunt, seated on his magnificent bay mare, blew the ancient Episcopalian call to slaughter, "YOICKS!," the barbaric sound caused a nearly insupportable agùe to rack his body while his complexion assumed the color of his sparkling new pink.

"I knew then it was no ordinary hunting horn," he often says, "and that to possess it was to possess the possibility of mastering the whole of pavilion music literature, one of my more public dreams." He will, at these times, occasionally rise as if in an excess of anxiety to survey unseeingly his collection of snowball lithographs, an expression of painful longing on his handsome, stupid face.

To master even a small portion of the vast literature of pavilion music has been the desire of all modern string players, especially those devoted to the rigors of the lute, dulcimer, viola da gamba, and stopped modess; no one has ever succeeded in performing more than competently in the literature on a horn, not even the greatest brass virtuosos. That Carmichael, a singer by profession, should have considered himself a candidate for such success and subsequent renown seems now like a bad joke, or as Sir Evelyn rather cruelly put it on a recent chipmunk shoot, "Haw, wot? Frightful!"

Recent information that Carmichael held numerous discussions with Dr. Robert Bedu makes his ambitions understandable if no more plausible. Dr. Bedu, it will be remembered, at the time the horn fell into Carmichael's hands, was about to conduct the final experiments with and trials of his harmonics inspissator, a small, mutelike apparatus designed to transpose instantly any score for any instrument or combination of instruments to a score for any other instrument or combination of instruments. The device was never marketed; whether Carmichael ever used an early prototype to attempt his scheme is unknown. The singer steadfastly denies ever having heard of a harmonics inspissator, and Dr. Bedu's interests have been focused, for some years now, on salad construction, and he refuses all interviews.

Whatever the truth, two things are definitely known of this murky period in Carmichael's decline. Whenever the tenor attempted to play even a single note of pavilion music—whether he had to hand the inspissator or not—the horn was utterly silent, despite all his efforts. However, did he casually pick up the horn and indifferently place it to his lips, the slightest exhalation of breath into the mouthpiece resulted in a shattering "YOICKS!" The unhappiness and frustration brought about by this state of affairs was, incidentally, the direct cause of his fiancée's departure, and her subsequent disastrous amour with Bridget Agostin, a woman whose erratic sexual behavior sometimes caused the birds to fall out of the trees.

A fascinating postscript to this story may be discovered in a recently completed report on an analysis of the horn, which unequivocally states that the instrument is *not made of silver* (but for the very rim of its bell), but of a thin, cheap alloy of the kind used, in the Depression, to make such mundane domestic items as beach pails, drying tableaux, cheese safes, breadboxes, and laundry hampers. The metal of the horn is, in the words of the report, "blue . . . so pale as to appear to be . . . silver to the naked eye."

⇒ SCARECROW ⇐

My Dear Chainville,

In the certain knowledge that your concern for and fascination with the shadowy events of the Past (if I may so egregiously simplify your long years of thought and research on the abyss of lost time) are as acute as ever, I thought it incumbent upon me to relate, briefly, a rather interesting occurrence of some three weeks ago.

I had been asked to Dr. Sydelle Lelgach's country retreat as a weekend guest, one of several, all of us having been invited at the behest of Dr. Lelgach's fiancé. He said something about the need she had—although she would not admit to it—for the distraction of conversation and laughter; apparently a troublesome case of monomania has been exhausting her time and intellectual energies. But this is neither here nor there.

On my first morning, a Saturday, I rose early and thought to take a walk in the neighborhood before breakfast. It was a windy, cloudy morning, just a little too warm for snow, and I set out across the fields at a good pace. After ten minutes or so, I saw, in a stubble field to my left, a scarecrow, but such a scarecrow as to make me instantly curious. I made my way to it, and as I approached, saw that it was made of the ordinary pair of rude tree limbs lashed together in the shape of a potence. However—and this is the element at once strange and familiar—a dirty black cloche and a tattered black slip comprised the figure's garments. I stood in weird expectation, seized by a sense of the uncanny, awaiting—how can I phrase it?— awaiting a revelation of some sort, while the wind buffeted the cloche and the slip fluttered and snapped.

Suddenly I remembered my mother, and the brief but strained scene we'd had upon the occasion of my informing her of my engagement to my late wife, Isabella. I remembered that she was about to leave for a dinner party and was dressed in a short black dress with spaghetti straps intended to show off her perfect shoulders, and a small black hat with a dotted half-veil. At the same moment, I heard her voice with lambent clarity: "So then nothing will dissuade you, Stephen, from marrying this tawdry Catholic?" A split second later, all was gone, all was as it had been, and I was alone with the scarecrow in the windy, silent field.

I wish to point out that the words which my mother spoke, and which, over the years, I had transformed into, "So then nothing will dissuade you, Stephen, from marrying this silly girl?," became clear only through the precise recollection of *my mother's apparel*, and it, in turn, had been called up by the bizarre spectacle of the female scarecrow. This phenomenon may be common, but not to me! I'd be pleased—and I am not a little anxious—to know what you think.

As ever,
Stephen Alcott

Stephen Alcott, the little-known author of difficult mystery novels, e.g., *The Soufflé Murders, Death Dines at Nine, Bloody Chocolate*, etc., whose gemlike surfaces and labyrinthine intricacies have endeared him to a small, discerning audience whose taste runs to the refinements of the baroque, has, for whatever reason, written a letter which falsifies the most important event of the morning he so carefully, if stiffly, describes. In truth, the important event was:

a blinding recollection of a strange woman, dressed in a dazzling white dress, or slip, who emerged from the darkness of a closet or cellar to speak to him, in his mother's voice, of the disappearance of his mother;

the woman looked exactly like his mother;

the woman stretched forth her hand;

the woman *was*, somehow, his mother;

he screamed in terror for *his* mother.

At this point, Alcott's memories faltered, began to fade, then ceased abruptly. He turned, troubled and distracted, toward the house. Glancing at the scarecrow, he saw the semblance of a face beneath the torn and dirty cloche, a face at once smiling and severe. The shadowy mouth opened: "So you're gonna marry the little cunt after all," it said.

❧ PRIEST ❧

On this dim, cold day, the church is almost empty. One man, beautifully dressed in a dark grey suit which is a perfect, if somewhat affectedly sober complement to the weather, kneels at the altar rail to receive the Eucharist.

The priest celebrant, when he was but nineteen, fell in love with Isabella Stella, a summer girl, as the locals would have surely termed her. The soft trochees of her name set him burning, darkly, darkly.

The priest, it seems, is *talking* to the worshiper, who looks up at him. But not in surprise.

Isabella's sister, Lona, was stupidly drowned in the shallows at the far side of the lake in a cruel and ominous accident just before Labor Day. The family left with Lona's body the day after her death, and the young man knew that Isabella would never again want to think about the lake or the summer or him. In time, he became a priest, surprising himself. Often, over the years, he would sit and look out the window, or at the wall. Thinking, perhaps, of deaths.

In the subtle evenings of that strange, murdered summer, Isabella wore a scent called White Sunset. It was fresh and breezy, deliciously dry and clean. The smell of sun-dazzled water and virgins.

The priest is talking to the worshiper, who is smiling up at him.

In the best tradition of melodrama, as our age understands melodrama, Isabella became the very image of an expensive prostitute, serving the arcane and exquisite aberrations of statesmen, diplomats, religious leaders, business executives, and celebrities of both sexes.

Now the priest is backing away from the altar rail, the chalice held, thoughtlessly, in his hand, his face flushed, his acolyte, in panic, looking about for assistance. But the church has in it but seven old women in black, oblivious to all but their God, the gentle vanguard of sweet death.

The man kneeling at the rail is, understandably, Isabella. Her brilliant androgyny has been of no small importance to her spectacular success as a fabled whore. To complete the sad fiasco, she wears White Sunset.

The priest stumbles and drops the chalice. The acolyte bursts into nervous tears, bewildered. Summer is months away.

⮞ LUST ⮜

The young woman at the window, her black hair pulled back in a severe chignon which dramatized her elegant profile, glanced at the paper in her hand, which looked, from a distance, to be an invoice or packing slip, or, perhaps, a bank statement. Later, it was ascertained, from an investigation of the tips hidden in, of all things, the aluminum soap dish, that it was, indeed, a bank statement. Jenny would much prefer to stay home this evening, so as to avoid the dinner party to which Ivan, her husband, has committed them. It will be the Provost, the Deans of Arts and Sciences and the Law School, their curiously blurred, smiling wives, and the Hounsfields: young Ivan, fine hard-working fellow, and young Jenny, lovely bright girl. Charming people to have on campus! Have you met the Hounsfields?, Dean Agostin will say, trying not to stare at Jenny's legs, his tongue barely protruding from between his tiny incisors.

A heavy wind drove a torrent of rain against the window-pane, and Jenny stepped back, startled. She closed the blinds and stood, annoyed, for a moment, then began unbuttoning her blouse, resigned to the evening and its predictable, alarmed gossip about the collapsing houses along the Old Arcade Road. She put the bank statement on the mantel, and tried out her generous, candid smile, then started for the bathroom. It was getting late.

Ivan was already dressed, save for his tie, and he sat in his study, leafing through a book of nineteenth-century freak cartoons. The materials discovered in the aluminum soap dish made no mention of this work, nor did any of the authorities seem to agree on precisely what freak cartoons were. Ivan looked carefully at them, frequently laughing quietly, a laugh which had, on certain intimate occasions, bewildered and chilled Jenny. He heard a noise, and looked up to see his wife, at the door, asking him something about a black dress she might wear, or should wear, or would like to wear. She was leaning against the door jamb, her blouse and brassiere in her hand. The narrow black skirt she wore accentuated her hips and the gleaming nudity of her upper torso. The light from the desk lamp slathered her breasts. Ivan stared at her, losing track of her language, hearing only soft noises, seeing a white smile. He was overwhelmed with lust, and rose from his chair, dropping his book on a round end table, from which it slid to the floor. He walked toward her, his hand reaching out; he could see in her face the dread of his massive desire.

Ivan then was brutally on top of her, his trousers tangled around his ankles, her torn panties twisted about her left knee, and he drove his hateful, stupid flesh into the secret, hairy wetness which makes her the rutting animal she is. He felt, again, as always, as if he was committing some terrible, unimaginable crime, some unspeakably delicious and unforgivable sin. It was Jenny's fault. Crazed, enraged, he stumbled into his orgasm, and turned his agonized face away from her wide eyes.

⇒ GNOMON ⇐

Dr. Sydelle Lelgach, a senior staff psychiatrist at the Pelepzin Hospital for the Criminally Insane, requested and was assigned Jonathan Tancred's case. Something different and complex beyond sociopathic pyromania attracted her to it. So she told her indifferent fiancé.

This attraction was heightened when she met Tancred for the first time. He was a slight, blond man, whose eyes, as if created by soothing cliché, had a fevered glint in them. He immediately took the doctor aback by complaining that he was not only troubled, but depressed, by his discovery that the hospital—which he obscurely referred to as "the blue hamper" —had, on one of its garden walls, a ponderous, concrete-and-bronze gnomon. As he spoke, he stared, with rude candor, at Dr. Lelgach's almost prim white blouse. "There are too many memories already, as you know," he said, "without having to accommodate those that a gnomon will attract." He closed his eyes. "And a slow gnomon!"

Dr. Lelgach waited for two weeks before she brought up the gnomon, and then, after a painfully resistant session during which Tancred returned again and again to what he called the "official-evidence faces" kept in malign readiness on the grounds, she asked him what he thought the gnomon had to do with memory. Tancred's eyes were fixed on the hem of her modest skirt, and, without looking up, he said, "Because it's what's left over, the gnomon. It's the remainder of a parallelogram after the removal of a similar parallelogram containing one of its corners. It's obvious!" he concluded, his voice rising. His stare shifted to her pale stockings, at which he gazed so intently that she felt a prickling of her calves and thighs. "Do you enjoy staring so vulgarly and openly at me?" she asked. Tancred gestured dismissively. "You *were* a virgin, but long ago. So why are you still wearing white underclothes?" Dr. Lelgach blushed, and, despite professional misgivings, ended the session. That afternoon, at the weekly staff meeting, she realized that she was compulsively tugging her skirt, again and again, over her knees.

A few days later, Tancred somehow set some paper afire and the ensuing blaze, before it was discovered, damaged his room rather severely. It was decided by the chief of psychiatry to keep the patient in security isolation until such time as he was considered to be, by the attending physician and observing staff, no longer a threat to himself and the other patients.

On the night of the chief's decision, Dr. Lelgach, looking through her mail at home, opened an envelope which bore the hospital's logo. Inside, executed with great care on a facial tissue, in what seemed to be ash or perhaps charcoal, was a drawing of a staring eye and the message: s, SEEN PARTS HEAL ME.

≫ BARNYARD ≪

This rustic figure standing in the meticulously designed barnyard of what he thinks of as his rural retreat, a farm in Bucks County, is Emiliano Soreau. It is good to get away from the feverish hustle, the hectic bustle—however exciting—of the publishing business. This is another of his maxims, one that the influential bookman will intone for the enlightenment of anyone in his employ. These chosen auditors invariably present to Mr. Soreau visages whose expressions combine sentiments of fealty, awe, fear, sycophancy, and hesitant camaraderie. Mr. Soreau is always deeply pleased, feeling, perhaps correctly, that he is thus in touch with the quotidian. On such occasions his dentures flash arcane leadership signals.

On this day, Mr. Soreau is dressed in the casual craftsman mode, i.e., a tall stovepipe cap, rather like a rough woollen kepi; a rugged canvas yard coat, suitably stained and frayed; well-worn corduroys; a faded engineer's neckerchief; and battered work boots. In his hand he holds a crusted pipe, and a mysterious metallic object, flowerlike in form, and indeterminate as to function, although rumor whispers that the object is a Heliotropic Seme Simplifier, one of a coveted few in the hands of major figures in the communications industry. Mr. Soreau's lips are pursed, as if to blow out a match or candle. Neither, it should be made clear, is in evidence, unless the metallic object is a match or candle in disguise. This seems unlikely. He might well be whistling, often an expression of executive satisfaction at how things (for instance) are going. "Things are going great guns!" is a phrase his subordinates love to hear. They await then, anxiously, the first white gleam of his terrifying smile.

Things *are* going great guns for the Soreau Communications Group (SoreCo), for Ström Owns, a hard-hitting personal journalist and actualist fictioneer—who can, on the strength of his latest book, *Cool Chill: The Death of the Avant-Garde*, write his own ticket—has agreed to do the story of Jonathan Tancred and the Book Inferno, or Word Blaze. This very morning, Mr. Soreau has received Owns's outline of the book, as well as a provisional list of chapter titles. These, in their acuity, have so pleased the distinguished publisher that he feels inclined to call Owns just to tell him how well they're going to get on together, like, perhaps, *great guns!* He grips his flowerlike object tightly, and stares into the bowl of his pipe, then purses his lips again. Soon, significant portions of his teeth may appear. He is truly delighted by the way that Owns, a remarkably *au courant* writer whose reportorial antennae are always operative, whose sense of the dramatic is always honed, has incorporated, as the chapter titles hint, some of the publisher's modestly proffered suggestions as to the book's concerns. Concerns and themes. Themes and direction. Direction and approach. The sweeping canvas, etcetera. Not that Mr. Soreau and his remarkable staff of *littérateurs* would interfere with a feverishly hustling, hectically bustling professional like Ström Owns. But the chapter titles do indeed seem to structure, is the word, structure the book almost *naturally!* If one can say that there is anything natural about a book!

Ha! Ha! Ha! Mr. Soreau laughs, and stares, cross-eyed, at his crusted briar again. So it *is* a briar. Suddenly, an authentic rustic, not to say pastoral breeze is produced from the electronic windcrafter within the barnlike command center before which the publisher, carefully grave now, stands.

1. Sudden Blunders; 2. A Tune Called "Heartaches"; 3. Call It Heroism; 4. A Dash of Cowardice; 5. Womanly Self-Sacrifice; 6. Icy Laughter; 7. Wild Tears; 8. Such Great Joy!; 9. Wrenching Agony; 10. Searing Questions; 11. Shocking Answers; 12. "Plain, Ordinary People"; 13. Sober Postmortems.

Owns has ended his letter by suggesting that the book might have in its title some reference to the fateful and tragic silver bugle that was blown so fatefully and tragically on that fateful yet tragic day. Perhaps something like *The Silver Bugle!* What does Mr. Soreau think?

Mr. Soreau thinks that he ought to get away to the country more often. The honest craftsman's life, that's the ticket! Or one of them. God knows, *money* doesn't mean anything. He has plenty of money. But crafting books alongside market-savvy master craftsmen! Ah! The breeze picks up, in accordance with the weekend environment-programming mode. And here comes another glowing smile!

⇒ COURTROOM ⇐

J. Branch Bex, like his brother, Caleb, an attorney, presents a pathetic figure in his rusty black robe and badly soiled white stock. And, also like Caleb, he is filled with vague regrets, crippled by repressions, and virtually overwhelmed by anxieties. These afflictions are not, however, pitiful enough to persuade his wife to return to him.

He stands at the defense table, overly excited and animated, as he always is when in court. His nondescript hat and battered briefcase—pointedly unopened—lie before him. His mouth, bright scarlet with the pralltriller lipstick (Red Dragon) he has taken to wearing on what he considers ceremonial occasions, is wide open, and with his right hand he gestures in the manner of someone lobbing a stick for a dog, perhaps, to fetch. From a coign of vantage, it can be discerned that one of the presiding justices is dozing, head in hand, and that another, the Chief Justice, lost in the pages of a semi-pornographic best-seller, *Suffocating Velvets,* is surreptitiously masturbating, in the grand tradition of the Superior First Circuit Court of Appeals— whose motto, *Dum vivimus, vivamus,* is, perhaps, pertinent in this instance. The other three justices are not visible, but are presumed to be present, more or less.

The case before the court is in is eighth month, and no one quite recalls its basic contours. Unforgettable testimony concerning stolen cycloidals and the Worcestershire-sauce creations favored by the admittedly depressed plaintiff is still belabored in the feature sections of countless daily rags; the most recent story, in the *Moray Plunger-Express,* rehashes the more scabrous elements of the case under the title "Family First?—Or Fur Coat Mania?," and is by the *Plunger-Express's* cultural editor, Ramp St. James, the media-proclaimed master of projection journalism.

Bex raises his voice, startling a quiet pigeon slowly dying of avian phthisis in the empty gallery: "Indeed, learned counsel for the prosecution, caught in the thick blue steel and organic rubbish of the so-called *facts*, wants you to believe that a *dark* cloche—as seen in the photograph that constitutes Exhibit G12 —is identical to a *black* cloche! One may as well believe it to be the mirror image of a glossy black Chinese teapot!"

"Order! Order, Mr. Bex!" the Chief Justice shouts, banging the gavel with his free hand, the corrosive elliptic of his piercing eyes commanding silence. "One more canting outburst and I'll hold you in contempt and sentence you to the open fields and dark trees of ruthless nature, flushed in lip and nail!"

Counsel for the prosecution hides his wind-up toy zeppelin, a scale model of the Navy's proud yet scandal-ridden U.S.S. *Football*, and wisely declines the court's invitation to comment, citing *Missouri* v. *Freaks*. Then Bex, spotting a woman who looks like Caleb in the last row, proceeds, in sudden perturbation, to ruin his client's case with what his father, Joshua, was pleased to denigrate as a "salad-dressing display," a form of specious argument and logic-chopping reminiscent of nothing so much as the ancient craft of juggling. But juggling, as Joshua would say, "only as corrupted by glorious bimbos in sheerest tights, highest heels, startlingest coiffures, winningest smiles, and inverted mordent lipsticks." The elder Bex would sometimes have trouble catching his breath as he inveighed against these practices, and no wonder, considering his precarious libido.

The woman who looks like Caleb is eating sugar cookies and marveling at the full-blown neuroses displayed by Branch. Although she doesn't know any of the Bex family, there is a possibility that this woman, about whose person there hangs the faint aroma of tea, would not be averse to being *compromised* by the Bexes! She certainly has the look of a woman who can find fulfillment only in a man, or several men, or a meaningful and creative career. Or enormous sums of money! She finishes her oddly shaped cookies and brushes the crumbs from her bosom to her lap and thence to the floor, in the timeworn gesture of women everywhere, even in the bush. At this time of day, the floor is rather filthy, yet the crumbs must go somewhere, of course, and to deposit them upon an already littered floor seems a sound idea. So. Troubled, she settles the model Packard sedan that is her constant companion, so to speak, in the placket of her strong, womanly skirt. The snow on her shoes has melted into a grey puddle on the floor—a homely touch amid the cold and rigid formality of the courtroom.

Bex is on his feet again, after having sat down in order to appease the momentarily dazed Chief Justice, whose entire body had been trembling in what is legally known as an "uncontrollable manner." Bex's mouth is open as before, hand gesturing as before. " 'Still summer afternoons!' or so my learned opponent has said. And 'deadly heat.' I accept these fragments of malarkey, but 'the sound of chickens clucking' is *not* evidence of the defendant's so-called fascination for the degenerate. That is a canard, speaking of poultry!" He sits again. There is a good possibility that no one has been listening very carefully to him. Still, the woman who looks like Caleb gives him a warm although not quite magnetic smile, and a glimpse of her little Packard.

≋ FOUNTAIN ≋

Although Verlaine does not describe his famous fountain, *this* fountain may well be its precise duplicate. So its description suggests. Verlaine's

> . . . sangloter d'extase les jets d'eau,
> Les grands jets d'eau sveltes parmi les marbres

is certainly not description, even though "sveltes" may be construed, with some misgivings, as a clue, at least, to the *look* of the fountain.

Verlaine's statues have no place at all in this setting, and their sites have been assumed by trees, that is, by descriptions of trees. These descriptions, carefully registered in a prose that is "at once precise and poetic," and dependent for its effects on "metaphor, symbol, analogy, allegory, and the like," include the information that behind one of the trees there is a woman, possibly in hiding. Her dress and chemise have been slipped off her shoulders and are gathered at her waist, and her bare breasts are streaming wet and soapy.

As she notices the importunate encroachments of the prose, she presses the palms of her hands, flat, over her nipples, and then, while clumsily attempting to maintain the concealment of her partial nudity, she begins to pull her disarrayed clothing over her upper torso. She is quite young, attractive, and svelte, but her face shows evidence of pain and anger: it is quite possible that she has recently been crying, for her face, also, is wet. It may be, of course, that she has been washing her face as well as her breasts, although, so the prose sees fit to mention, her face is soapless.

Her recent crying is remarked upon in a note to the description of the hidden woman (*n.b.*, yet another search of the duplication of the scene—with the noted statuary substitutions kept in mind—which has given rise to the highly praised precise, poetic, metaphorical, symbolic, analogous, allegorical language, reveals that the woman is *not present*, but that all indications point to the possibility that she is, indeed, *hiding* behind one of the trees), to the effect that in Dowland's song, "Weepe you no more sad fountaines," the fountains referred to are discovered to be the lover's eyes.

Perhaps the fountain bequeathed to us by Verlaine has something to do with the weeping eyes, the sad fountains, of the hidden woman! It may be that Verlaine, composing "Clair de Lune," had Dowland in mind, and that the later poet's fountain occurred as an unconscious metaphor for the invisible young woman's weeping eyes. The phrase "sangloter d'extase" is thus clarified.

The descriptive prose pokes around behind the trees, which quietly rustle near the "jets d'eau sveltes," but the woman is nowhere to be found. The prose describes, and yet again describes, but to no avail. The woman is, simply, not there.

Perhaps she never left her bathroom at all, although her son swears that she disappeared forever. At least for him.

➢ FLASHLIGHT ❦

In the era that the Mammoth Spectacular Corporation, in its glossy promotional brochures, chooses to call the Diamond Days of Laughter!, Jed Whag stood at the very peak of his profession as clown and juggler. This position was reached some few years before he met the dissolute and irresistible Ann Jenn, for whom the world, as a society reporter of the time wrote, was a cheap bracelet. The ensuing scandal, centered in street events of a sensational nature—made more sensational by rumor—destroyed his career, of course, as well as the careers, and sometimes the lives, of many others.

In a recent burst of depraved nostalgia for the fifties, a decade of such paranoia, guilt, hysteria, destruction, and gloom that it is now, quite predictably, thought of as an age of innocence, Whag's more famous acts have been the talk of the Modern Living and Today's Arts sections of myriad newspapers. It is rather pleasant, for those who remember Whag in his heyday, to be reminded of his performances and the unique mania that energized them.

Among his most notable comedy routines, played, most usually, in elaborate costume under a single, intensely bright spotlight, were The Demented Canoeist, Leaking Gazebo, The Nun's Washcloth, Lost Missal, The Moon Adventure, The Thing on the Floor, Drunken Sculptor, The Bellowing Pussy, Fallen Balloon, and The Yellow-Brown Fowl. In his capacity as nonpareil juggler, or, as he was billed, JESTER JED THE JEWEL OF JUGGLERS, feature writers invariably recall three of his feats: one, in which he juggled an open straight razor, a rotten canteloupe, a garden hose, a gallon jug of whiskey, and a kitchen sink; a second revealed his skills as addressed to a leaky hot-water bottle, a Philadelphia lawyer, a sad fountain, a silver bugle, and *A la recherche du temps perdu*; and a third displayed his finesse with a case of phials, a short black dress, a classic arbalest, a Harlow Warbucks life-sized doll, and an assistant editor.

Another story unearthed from that frenzied age is the one told—and told again!—by Whag's valet, concerning his employer's nocturnal searches—dressed in rough clothes and armed with a powerful flashlight—for items and elements and ideas out of which he might create even more stunning performances. The valet, who was not precisely a slave to accuracy, maintained that Whag had occasionally mentioned some of the things for which he searched, and that among them were a translucent spheroid, official memories, pavilion music, zeppelin silhouettes, idol tears, a white figure, and a thesel. It is rather unlikely that Whag would confide in his valet, especially concerning his work, about whose conception, development, and refinement he was fanatically secretive. Be that as it may, if the valet's story can be given any credence whatsoever, it is probable that Whag was about to ascend to a plane, at once surreal, abstract, and ominous, never before assayed by any performer, if Whag may be labeled a mere performer.

The scandal put an end to all this, and the unrevealed evidence of monstrous depravities that the district attorney's office held in threatening abeyance quite effectively stymied any hope that Whag may have desperately entertained concerning a comeback or even a formal farewell appearance. It is rumored that he still walks the night with a flashlight, moving quietly through the thick, depressing fogs of his chosen place of exile.

⧉ OBJECT ⧉

Here is a strange object, supposedly found in a remote but interesting landscape by a rather distinguished woman, who, understandably, does not wish her identity revealed. Her name is Queen, so they say, and many of her days by the window are filled with weeping, some of it unforgivable. Queen, of course, is not her real name.

At present, it rests on *terra incognita*, or a beach, although panels of independent experts are in disagreement as to the *legitimacy* of the beach (or *terra incognita*). That is, certain schools of thought insist that the *terra incognita* (or beach) is but a *facsimile*, of the kind constructed by the Art Millionaire Workers Collective, made—not to put too fine a point on it—to sell and sell quickly. "Homage to Andy" seems to be, in this case, the well-known ticket, usually verbalized as "it's out there, so let's get ours!" A healthy vulgarity may surely be allowed its moment, after all.

Women, as usual, have little part in all this, although, to be just, there are certain cliques designated, often militantly, for women only. Texts prove this. The men are secretly delighted by these events, and grumble about this segregation quite wonderfully and convincingly when the cameras are on them, although "cameras" is, here, purely metonymic. Otherwise, the sexes are up to their old tricks, e.g., there are the hurt feelings, false orgasms, stale quarrels, "love locked out in all the cold and rain," etc. Everyone, more or less, remembers *that* old song. How it echoes across the dismal lake!

In any case, it looks like a hot-water bottle, albeit with small, oddly shaped nipples here and there on its surface. Queen was, at first, somewhat disturbed by this, but there has not been much concern shown for her wishes since the moon incident. It is, definitely, a *rather poor symbol* (for which there is still a small, but steady demand by the loyal minority). There has been some genial banter concerning its suitability for vast lofts, most especially those owned by artists who think nothing of courageously calling the status quo into question. Projection techniques have made it possible to image large throngs filing religiously by the object with that charming blend (or mixture) of awe, envy, and hatred that characterizes the suspicious appreciator.

On the other hand, no one has ever actually *seen* the object. All that is available for scrutiny is a drawing of the object—really a photostatic copy of a reproduction of a drawing—so that it is possible to maintain, with a handful of cynics, that the curious object (or hot-water bottle) does not exist, except as, of course, an image's image imaged, existent but in two dimensions, and paltry ones, at that. Critics, aware of admittedly popular trends, argue that such an image falsifies the object to such a degree that one may as well study a photostatic copy of a reproduction of a drawing of, for example, a *large turkey*, as have a photostatic copy of a reproduction of a drawing of a strange object. "Photostatic," in this case, may be understood to function within the same linguistic code as "beach." So all becomes increasingly problematic.

It may thus be seen that on selected metalinguistic levels, art is, after all, *not much.* Yet who, of all those brave tyros, would have guessed this? When the notion was broached at a meeting of the Collectors Association, there ensued a loud and collective "Hurrah!" Strange objects, and, for that matter, art in general, should be understood *in perspective:* so the argument went. The burden of the major address focused on highly collectible images of a debased world in which peepholes are discovered in the walls of ladies' restrooms and/or dressing rooms. These victimized, or potentially victimized women, it was pointed out, could well be, or could well have been, or well might be, or are, wives and daughters and sisters and mothers! The disguised message given the enthusiastically applauding audience of the intelligent affluent was, to put it quite bluntly, "Shit to art!" There are still, it seems, traditional standards.

Yet the object (or its image as imaged as imaged) persists. What memories it might reveal could it but talk! And perhaps, sterile sands (or beach) aside, it *will*.

Some liquid, by the way, constantly spills onto the beach (or *terra incognita*) from the object, an event noticed by absolutely no one. Of course, it may not actually be liquid. Recalling the theoretical positions which currently hold sway, it may well be *molten blue metal*, arguably, a kind of fog.

⇒ INSULT ⇐

Disputes over the precise nature of the insult have been simmering for some time, and those privy to the many meetings and conferences—some formally arranged, others spontaneous and *de facto* gatherings of interested parties, e.g., historians, gossips, celebrity seekers, popular-culture savants, journalists, youthful academics, aspiring large-audience novelists, market analysts, serious sports fans, and others—agree, for the most part, at least at certain times of the year, on the difficulty of ascertaining the facts, or even some of the facts. That Cassandra Ballesteros has designated herself an interim expert on the affair has hardly helped, especially since her supposed entanglement in what has become known as "l'affaire Chainville." The focus of virtually everything, Frank (Meat Czar) Hector himself, has, regrettably, been a sour recluse for many years, and is said to have destroyed whatever documentation may once have existed. Not, of course, that documentation, however meticulous, would have served anyone's purposes.

The essentials of the incident are well known, and, indeed, have come to assume the status of modern legend. On a mild evening in May, some twenty years ago, Frank Hector entered the foyer of Le Crépuscule Nellie, at the time the newest and most exciting casino on the Strand. Like all parvenus, he was dressed too carefully: swallowtail coat, striped trousers, wing collar, black cravat, and in his hand the inevitable gold-headed stick gripped covetously. His retinue, scattered before and behind him, either did not see or paid no heed to the man who suddenly confronted Hector to thrust a small white card at him. This individual, dressed in the exact manner as the rich butcher, was ushered from the Crépuscule's foyer by Hector's irritated bodyguards, but not before he'd had the opportunity to observe the fear and disgust which took possession of the usually inane visage of the abattoir tycoon.

It is concerning this point that the disputes begin. Bolstered by opinions derived from Lacanian psychoanalysis, vaginal politics, market-destruct economics, neo-post-deconstructionist ur-theory, codified phrenology, quantum heteroclosure formalism, revisionist sombrerism, gender calculus, cafeteria mechanics, and repression theology, the disputants have variously argued that the card was blank, that it held a small mirror, that it was actually a heat-activated spinach camera, that it was a photograph of Mrs. Hector and three Russian sailors enacting a spiritedly fevered version of the Safranski quartet, etc., etc. There is not a scintilla of evidence to support any of these conjectures.

Recently, a medium claiming to be the common-law widow of one of the bodyguards who attended Mr. Hector on that curious evening released to the tabloid press the preposterous information that the card contained the following message:

Chitterlings at the sink, kitchen dim. Hocks, tin pig behind the door. Cold backyard. Cheesehead untied, steak. Shoes. Man steps on tongue, light. Over! Glaring legs, sunset, tails, blue metal hampers. Veal, glass bathroom. Sweetbreads, zeppelin, calves. White ribs and spare dresses, and boiling on the London stairs.

The medium is quoted as saying that "her darling's, God bless him, voice sounds a little phlegmy, but really sincere!"

The only other information at least partially verifiable is the account which attests that Hector, after composing himself, thrust the card into his pocket, entered the casino, and, gambling recklessly, lost heavily at baccarat. He also gave his hat away to an authoritative young woman severally described as a corporation lawyer, transmission slut, plastic surgeon, pert gamin, veteran reporter, and laudatory whore. These descriptions are ascribed to Cassandra Ballesteros, whose pretensions have already been touched upon, and who has never been thought of as one to revere the truth. That said, however, it should be admitted that her buffets are famous for their imitation meatballs, many of which have been designed by notable artists.

⟫ RECITAL ⟪

Although it was apparent that the scandal was just about to become public knowledge, Russell Cuiper, who, according to fairly reliable if shadowy witnesses, was thoroughly enmeshed in the unsavory affair, decided to give, as scheduled, his renowned violin program for the usual group of *divertissement* lovers. It was, of course, his last performance, although no one could have known that at the time. There were, *after the fact,* the pundits who pretended to have been, all along, suspicious because of Cuiper's absent piano accompanist, a young woman who played mechanically and sang in a distant, faltering soprano. Cuiper had often played solo, and on this night he brought off the program with élan, even though silent protesters in the rear of the recital hall held up signs which read, variously, GYNOCRACY IS OKAY; FIDDLES—WHILE BABIES STARVE?; and ART IS A BOURGEOIS TRICK.

Cuiper, seeming isolate on stage because of the unplayed score propped up on the piano, was what one scowling reviewer described as "a cliché incarnate: white tie, slightly long, carefully wild hair, grave face, eyes closed in concentration—all testified to his mastery of time-honored art codes." The audience, musical amateurs in the very best sense of the word, was satisfactorily enthralled by the performance. A kind of dangerous tension, engendered by the irregular circumstances, hung over the intimate hall, and the violin—muted, as always, with a lucky matchbook from the Enamel Club—projected a somber if undemanding beauty that drifted almost slothfully among the crowd. It was precisely as if the rumors concerning the accompanist, rumors which did not surface for at least a week after the recital, were in the air that very night!

The most persistent of these rumors had it that the accompanist was the heiress, Ann Jenn, herself; that she had missed the performance because of a contretemps with a number of radical Evangelists to whom she had intentionally and maliciously exposed herself; that the police, arriving at the scene, dared not arrest the woman who, quite literally, owned them, even though one witness called her behavior before the officers "astonishingly lewd." An addendum to and variation on this story declared that Miss Jenn was, indeed, placed under arrest, but that her identity was revealed when the arresting officers searched her handbag and discovered, among her wadded-up underclothes and a small box of translucent spheroids, her driver's license, stamped, incidentally, "NOT VALID." However farfetched such stories, it cannot be denied that the scandal broke but a month or so later, bringing down the Clean Marriage movement, and wrecking the careers of at least four senators, three of them solid family men with Christian drinking problems and affinities for hearty cross-dressing or pubescent boys.

Since Russell Cuiper no longer plays, it may be of some interest to the lay historian of light-classical music, or, as it is sometimes called, "mellow sounds," to have a list of the songs played at the final recital. Some of the titles reveal the hand of Ann Jenn or of her paramour by correspondence, Jed Whag, the forgotten man:

"Woman at Her Sponge Bath"; "Cuisine Noire"; "A Distant Voice"; "Empty Patio"; "Child's Footsteps"; "Man in the Distance"; "Hard Light and Flat Surface"; "Cold Twilight"; "Wardrobe, a Study in Blue"; "Impenetrable Portal"; "Small Airship"; "Virgin Trio à la Snow."

⇝ BARREL ⇜

The legendary clarinet virtuoso, Sandor Skariofszky, whose famous mechanical interpretation of Satie's recently discovered "Entracte pour les blanches entractes rag" fills him— the very *thought* of it fills him—with nausea, has, in recent years, taken to saving coins in a bank shaped like a miniature barrel, which he carefully displays on his mantelpiece. To say that he saves coins does not begin to cover the appealing and even irresistible events which make up Skariofszky's days. There are, of course, the stationery sprees, fox-trot contests, sycophant correspondence, and daily visits to Old Tony, the cheerful Italian bootblack, whose irreverent tales of the Piedmont and its lusty mountain women and their amorous swains belie his cherished notion that everyone is, underneath, really homosexual. All these avocations suffuse the jaded musician with dreams of a permanently simple yet zesty life. Then there are, too, the gambling orgies, the jacket (and topcoat) fittings, and the embouchure exhibitions. Yet it must be admitted that the woodwind star finds his true fulfillment in the coin-saving ritual to which he has submitted himself.

The master indulges in the ritual whenever he looks at a certain picture on that wall perpendicular to the one into which the fireplace is built. The pattern is, of needs, well, perhaps not of *needs*, fixed: Skariofszky approaches the picture, as if casually and by accident, stops, studies it with care, turns, moves in four strides to the mantel, hovers above the little barrel—which Old Tony, strong white teeth gleaming in his wonderfully swarthy face, refers to as a "sangaweech"—and, with his right hand, deftly drops a coin into the bank's slot. During this operation, Skariofszky's left arm is bent rigidly at his side and his left hand clenched in a threatening fist. At such times, the clarinet wizard resembles Bart Ballesteros, whose pathetic suicide stunned the croquet world. He is *not* Bart

Ballesteros, however, because he is, most assuredly, he; and because Ballesteros's response to the visual—despite family lies to the contrary—was wholly devoid of either taste or understanding. He had, as the Romanian proverb puts it, "the glass eye which [has] cracked [up] among pebbles."

Something draws him to the picture, again and again, obsessively and exhaustingly. His left arm has long since begun to atrophy, his left hand may never fully open again, and his staring, dark-ringed eyes are cruelly bloodshot. At times, his admirers, members of the international Licorice Clubs, deplore the fact that he no longer performs, and his frustrated physicians concur, filling the air with their professional rodomontade concerning creative therapeutics and other schemes designed to encourage cheeriness. Skariofszky pays them no heed. He has even ceased to treat them with courtesy.

There is, by the way, nothing exceptional about the picture. A rather brilliant imitation of the Hudson River School, it depicts, beneath an unsettled, stormy sky, a dark lake. At its far end, there can barely be descried the figures of three young women in wide straw hats and luminous white dresses, wading in the shallows, their full skirts held modestly close to their perfect thighs. They appear to be dead.

☞ CASINO ☜

The Enamel Club was internationally renowned as the casino that permitted to play only those who no longer knew how to do anything else but gamble. The atmosphere of the club was, as might be imagined, raw, electric, and suffused with danger and bleak despair. Men bought chips with markers backed by their failing businesses and unattended investments, their cars and houses; women pledged their wardrobes, credit accounts, and children; and those the club managers deemed attractive enough were permitted to endorse vouchers promising future sexual labors for periods of up to five years of what would be, in fact, indentured prostitution. That lives were constantly being destroyed filled the casino with a thrilling and reckless energy, and awestruck, voyeuristic visitors were quite willing to pay absurdly high fees simply to watch the action on the floor. Many of them, pale and trembling and sticky with cold sweat, had to be helped to their cars or rooms after an hour or two of watching the gamblers in their hopeless ecstasy.

The main gambling room, with tables for craps, roulette, blackjack, faro, chemin de fer, and baccarat, was not unlike such rooms everywhere, although the remarkable mullioned windows on three sides of the room—each framed by richly brocaded drapes—and the silver Louis XIV lamps hanging over each table, served to make the Enamel Club unique. This special ambience, this sophisticated setting for pervasive disaster, was broken one night, at the very moment that a middle-aged man at the roulette table had signed over his wife so as to be able to cover his bets on IMPAIR.

As other players put down their bets, there was discerned a commotion under the table, directly beneath the wheel itself. The croupier quickly lifted the heavy felt tablecloth to reveal a young man, dressed obstreperously—and incorrectly!—in a green tweed suit, Tyrolean hat, and brogans, mounted atop a woman almost twice his age, whose evening gown, a classic Balenciaga, was understandably disheveled. They were copulating in single-minded frenzy, and at the moment that the croupier exposed them to the crazed stares of players and onlookers, had reached a mutually delirious *jouissance*, the lengthy duration and accompanying howls of which caused several ruined gamblers to collapse with the carnal jitters.

The police were, of course, called, and the offending couple arrested on a battery of misdemeanor charges. The young man, it turned out, was Ivan Hounsfield, a highly thought-of staff member at the nearby university, and his partner, Bridget Agostin, was the community-oriented wife of Martin Agostin, the Dean of the College of Arts and Sciences at the same university. Mrs. Agostin, after hurriedly donning some scattered garments that she referred to, three or four times, as having been "misplaced," completely covered her head with Hounsfield's moortramper handkerchief. She insisted, even in the face of the numerous items of identification that the police found in her bag, that she was Mrs. Rufus Packard, a visiting nutritionist. She also repeated three sentences over and over again: "My Spanish, sirs, is passing good, sí," "I surely must have fainted, kind officers," and "I've never laid eyes on him before!"

This blatantly crude and misdirected adventure on Ivan's part did not precisely ruin him, but relations between him and the Dean became, and remained, extremely strained, his raises would be, for years to come, minuscule, and his hopes for promotion futile. Being the essential lout that he was, he blamed his wife for everything that had happened, even for the holes he had torn in the knees of his hideous tweeds.

Most pointedly, however, this seriocomic interlude changed, irreversibly, the Enamel Club, and it never again regained its cachet of potential doom. It became, simply, another casino—and one with a bawdy tale attached. Even the casino's distinctive and coveted matchbooks were, after a time, no longer coated with glossy black enamel, perhaps the truest indication of the club's descent into the banal.

⇒ NOTE ⇐

There was a period during which Dr. Sydelle Lelgach's fiancé was everywhere seen with his heavily bandaged right hand in a sling, his weight supported by a cane, carried in—of needs—his left hand. He also affected a false moustache which made him look, by some quirk of physiognomy, vaguely unhinged. To all who asked about his injury, he offered sundry variations on one of two stories: that he had been operated on for an encysted ganglion; that he had injured himself, in his capacity as a chief hydrological engineer, while working on a variant model of the autorobotic electro-digital water box. Both of these stories were false. The young man had actually broken his wrist and most of the bones in his right hand as the result of his smashing his fist repeatedly against Sydelle's kitchen wall. This show of fury was caused by his exasperation with her increasingly strange behavior: and she was not only acting strangely, she was wholly unaware of the fact that she was acting strangely. When her fiancé called her attention to some oddity of conduct which she had never before displayed, Sydelle would become enraged and accuse him of "hysterical verbalization *à la* Jung!"

Among the more notable aberrations to which she seemed in thrall may be counted her tugging down the hem of her skirt whenever she was seated; the glances she'd direct at rumpled slips of paper pulled from her pockets or handbag while otherwise engaged in conversation; the almost weekly complaints she'd make of illnesses to which she swore she had fallen victim —amoebic dysentery, smallpox, poliomyelitis, yellow fever, diphtheria, cirrhosis, acquired immune deficiency syndrome, beriberi, multiple sclerosis, and many others. She also drew, over and over again, a sketch of what could be considered as either a stylized target or an eye; and she referred to her clothing, no matter what she wore, as one kind of costume or another. Perhaps her most egregious and unsettling behavior was exhibited at dinner on the evening when she first met her fiancé's mother and two older sisters. A general question on psychoanalysis had been put to Sydelle by one of the sisters, the sort of question which asks no answer but a smile, or, at most, an innocuous and virtually contentless reply. Her fiancé never could, afterward, quite recall the question, because the shock of Dr. Lelgach's answer silenced—and brought to a flustered conclusion—the dinner party. "In the final analysis, pun intended, all schizophrenic behavior has to do with cocks or cunts," she said with cool dignity.

And then, finally, there was the sudden news delivered to him by an old friend, concerning Stephen Alcott and his intrusion into Sydelle's life: Stephen Alcott, that insufferable, that intolerable hack! He couldn't believe it. He *wouldn't* believe it! But one day Sydelle showed him a handful of Polaroid snapshots taken in what a night-table ashtray identified as the Blue Bird Inn. They were utterly shameless, and he turned to her, furious, hurt, humiliated, but before he could speak, she looked at him pathetically and announced that she had contracted typhus.

One afternoon, soon after, while he fought with himself over his insulted desire for her, still, and in the face of his realization that she had become somebody else, he arrived at her apartment to take her to lunch, but found the place empty. On the table was a note.

I'll be fucking Steve probably all afternoon, so if you're hungry, make yourself something to eat. Plenty of cold beer.
love, Sydelle
P.S. *MANE ΘΕΣΕΛ ΨΑΡΗΣ*

It was then that he began punching the wall. Tiny drawings of staring eyes came fluttering down from the shelves above the sink.

In the hurt yet cavalier letter that she wrote to him some two months later, in tardy reply to his silence and absence, she asserted that the Greek postscript means "this is a joke" or

"I'm only joking." But her fiancé, weeks earlier, had discovered that the letters convey no message, that they mean nothing at all, that the so-called Greek is no more than an illusionless cartoon, no more than the empty center of the ubiquitous eyes.

⤷ DOMINOES ⤶

Marcus Tommie, the departmental supervisor, had begun to suffer strange blackouts, or, as he thought of them, headaches, after which he had difficulty trusting in the ability of language to represent reality, or, for that matter, even small parts of it. He began, uncharacteristically, to frequent cafés and restaurants in the evenings, hoping that such an attempt at relaxation, or recreation—a word that upset him—might aid in ridding him of these dislocating experiences.

One night, he struck up an acquaintance with a man his own age, and after a light meal together, they decided to walk down the street to a café to share a bottle of wine and play dominoes, the only game, save for Napoleon Whist Casino, that Mr. Tommie liked. He often said that he found the tiles refreshingly Jewish, although he never explained what he meant by this phrase.

He and his newfound acquaintance played for some time amid congenial small talk fostered by a fine bottle of claret. Suddenly, Mr. Tommie's companion picked up a tile and, staring at it, asked Mr. Tommie to look around the room, which the puzzled supervisor did.

"Do you see anything out of the ordinary?" his companion asked. "Anything that looks a little odd or out of place?" Mr. Tommie looked around again, very carefully, but for some reason his temples had begun to hurt and he found it impossible to concentrate. He shook his head.

"Those bowls, placed haphazardly about the room," his companion began, "are filled with translucent spheroids made of the same material as these tiles! I *thought* they were unique. Such superb translucency is rarely encountered, especially in spheroids."

Mr. Tommie nodded, his mind beginning to slip off the man's words into a threatening but weirdly comfortable murk.

He looked glassily at a bowl of the shining globes on a nearby sideboard.

"The reason I remark on this," the man said, "is because these spheroids bring to mind a strange experience, one to which I've never quite reconciled myself." Mr. Tommie nodded again, the phrase "enameled rouge manqué" presenting itself to him with great clarity.

His companion then, without preamble, told him the following story. One hot afternoon, many years before, when he was about fifteen, he had wandered through dense trees to the edge of a dark, cool lake. Hearing voices and laughter, he looked down the shoreline and discovered three girls, about his age or a little older, wading in the blue shadows. All three were in identical white bathing suits, and they were performing the most astonishing feats of juggling with dozens of different-colored balls of an unearthly translucency. Their genius was remarkable, and they easily brought off such difficult accomplishments as the fan-tan stroll, the harp dreamer, and the well-nigh impossible *spiritus mundi*. He watched the girls for perhaps a half hour, after which time two of them collected all the balls, climbed onto the grassy bank, and dried themselves. The third girl, a beauty with black eyes and hair, calmly sank into and then under the water, where she seemingly drowned herself, while her companions ate lunch over a batch of movie magazines. He splashed into the water and waded toward the submerged girl, but by the time he reached her, she was dead. He looked toward the shore, but there was no sign of the other girls—there was no sign of anything.

The man stopped talking and looked expectantly at Mr. Tommie, who stared at him and said, "In opaquely future, priests or cottages white dresses small, altar." He frowned and nodded. "Black windows kitchen, decidedly, or cold?" he concluded.

"Of course," the other man said, "I could have been dreaming, as you seem to suggest, but why then would the 'dream' spheroids be *here*, in this particular café, to which we have come by chance?"

Mr. Tommie smiled mechanically, and wondered if the steadily increasing pain in his head could possibly grow strong enough to kill him, or if that was too much to hope for.

⊰ COLLOQUY ⊱

The lights come up to reveal a bare stage, upon which stand three figures. In the foreground is an OFFICER *in a grey uniform, at attention, his eyes covered by a large white blindfold. His back is to a pair of* SOLDIERS *in blue uniforms, who have placed themselves slightly behind and to either side of him. They are armed with rifles, which they hold rather casually upright, butts resting on the floor. The* SOLDIERS *stare past the* OFFICER *at what may be thought of—for want of a better word—nothing.*

OFFICER: Despite temporary exigencies, and the realization that the analyst's desire to listen to the analysand's fruitless inventions is a sublimation of voyeurism, everything follows the path of the zeppelin.

SOLDIER 1: If he were a woman, she'd stand at a grimy window and expose herself to the neighbors. Sculpture of a religious nature is no cure for such behavior, despite the recent findings of expert art committees.

SOLDIER 2: One of my own favorite songs is "Valencia," as both of you well know. It has a *sunny* sound to it, which can remind one of beach pavilions. Cool lakes, the smell of hamburgers, the damp, sandy floor. Other summery items.

SOLDIER 1: *Exempli gratia,* the persistent records on the jukebox, all of which, save for "Valencia," slip my mind.

OFFICER: I played alto saxophone one summer, many years ago. Speaking of music. I recall a certain Lona, whose white teeth were brilliant against the deep tan of her lovely face. Her bathing suit was multicolored. Wide pastel stripes, vertical, as I remember. She drowned. Certain letters were written about her in no-nonsense prose.

SOLDIER 1: Were the hearts of the correspondents in the letters? Shall I explain that hoary figure?

OFFICER: Yes. No.

SOLDIER 1: Had Lona lived, she may have become the invaluable yet uncelebrated accompanist to a famed musical charlatan. On the other hand, one never knows.

OFFICER: Narcissism was probably her style, more up her alley, as they say. I once asked her for a token of her affection, a garment, for instance, suitable for concealment about my person and as an aid in masturbatory fantasies in what I knew would be my lonely trench. Or bunker.

SOLDIER 2: And?

OFFICER: She indicated a tree, located by the handball courts! Her sister, Isabella, winked at me. A born whore.

SOLDIER 1: And Isabella's fate?

OFFICER: Lost in the echoing vastness of the hollow years, sort of. Yet her grit and determination, coupled with her insane belief that one can be whatever one wants to be, may have stood her in good stead in the demandingly optimistic worlds of business, academe, and, well, other demandingly optimistic worlds. In the hurly-burly and bustle and hustle of the work-aday and its varied perversions. Still and all, she may well have been a failure, like the rest of us.

SOLDIER 2: These remarks are quite similar to those you've recently been accused of making about Nadja, are they not?

OFFICER: They are most assuredly not! And may I suggest that Nadja has no place in this discussion? The blue of your uniforms, by the way, fellows, is very close to the blue of metal laundry hampers. At least those that I remember. I admit that it's hard to remember anything that occurred in the pre-traumatic years. One does recall a dark picture in a hallway, though. Distant female figures, in white.

SOLDIER 1: The trauma, as you call it, didn't prevent you from ogling the women who came to you for advice, military and otherwise.

SOLDIER 2: Even though your defense is that the trauma begat the ogling, a sophistical or something, if I ever heard one.

OFFICER: But I *have* successfully excised certain offensive words from my rough-and-tumble soldier's vocabulary, that you must admit, and you be honest! For instance, "cripple" and "Miss." Also "masquerades," "loony," "broad," "lips," and "friend."

SOLDIER 1: Not to spoil anything, but I'm out of ideas for now, and feel that my joyously declarative sentences have just about done their rattling good job.

SOLDIER 2: Thank you. And may I say that they've been the sort of sentences that make one realize that meaning, and finding a place in youths' hearts are what it's all about. Now, I must note that this small play, called, for unknown reasons, *Balloon*, has often been performed alone—as now—or as one of a pair of one-act plays, its varied partners usually written by new voices in the theatre. However, historically, *Balloon* was intended as a kind of dramatic preparation for the legendary melodrama *The Deranged Ones*.

OFFICER: Surely one of the jewels in the hat of modern drama.

SOLDIER 1: Thought of by many of our most thoughtful critics, actually, as the hat itself.

SOLDIER 2: It's time for the lights to go out as abruptly and theatrically—ha! ha!—as they came up.

BLACKOUT

Notes: Balloon is often performed alone or as one of a pair of one-act plays, although it was originally written as a kind of introduction to Nadja's seminal surrealist drama *The Deranged Ones*. It was recently performed at the memorial service for Bart Ballesteros, long a friend of the theatre. Edward Carmichael played the Officer; Gregory Balbet, Soldier 1; and Stephen Alcott, Soldier 2. Those in attendance familiar with the play have asserted that almost all of the dialogue was garbled.

⇒ BOOK ⇐

Cassandra Ballesteros, whose considerable sensuality has not been lost on Ström Owns, a rural fop given to dreams of literary fame as a chronicler of our time, has suggested to the rube that a certain book, much in demand, is how she phrases it, by Donald Chainville, may also hold *some interest* for others. She smiles as she says this, her snowy teeth glistening in the seductive lamplight. She crosses her legs, languorously, her stockings electrically whispering. Owns's eyes bug out rather comically, although records indicate that he felt anything but comical. The flesh is, as always, ludicrous.

Needless to say, Owns is in Chainville's study the next day, his hands slowly opening the book which may contain the information that will, perhaps, gain him Cassandra's favors. He flushes as he thinks of them in all their possible varieties. All he needs is the *key passage!* Oddity, however, looms, as it will, and almost immediately. The intrepid lout discovers that the text of the book is printed on the recto of each leaf, the verso being blank. All the pages are uncut, and the text's illustrations, inside, so to speak, the uncut pages, are, of needs, invisible to the casual browser. It is somewhere among these illustrations, sequestered in the "inside out" Japanese binding, that the clue to the correct passage—according to the maddening Cassandra—can be discovered.

Seated rigidly at Chainville's desk, and, it should be remarked, wearing his clothes, Owns, since he dares not cut the pages, carefully pulls them open, and begins meticulously to inspect the black-and-white illustrations. His heart begins to flutter sickeningly as he realizes that the illustrations, each one captioned with a line supposedly taken from the text, have nothing to do with the text; nor do the captions. In a stupor of lubricious despair, Owns pages through the book, looking at the robustly academic illustrations, and reading, in bewilderment, the remarkable captions, here reproduced in the interests of justice, a somewhat obscure phrase:

DESPERATELY, THE SULTAN FELL TO A RUGGED KNEE; THEY WERE HALF-CLOTHED BUT JOVIAL TO A FAULT; "HE'S AN ODD-LOOKING CHUMP," THE SLUT MOCKED; THE LAD WOULD SOON FIND THE CITATION AT THIS RATE!; TIME FOR THE LAMPS TO BE CHOKED; ERRANT AUTUMN BREEZES?; NOW SHE WAS THE BOSS!; "THE OLD TREE SEEMS LONELY," THE HIKER ENTHUSED; HE HAD ATTAINED THE WINTRY SUMMIT DESPITE HIS ILL-FITTING CAP; IT SEEMED TO BE AN ENORMOUS CAN OF SOUP; DESPERATELY, THE HUNTSMAN BLEW THE HOUNDS' TUNE; IT LOOKED VERY LIKE A SISSY SCARE-CROW; THE MAN AT THE ALTAR RAIL BURST INTO FLAMES!; MELISSA HAD, INDEED, BEEN DRAFTED; "SO THIS IS THE FAMOUS TOWN GNOMON," ZOE CHUCKLED; OLD PIERRE WAS AFRAID OF WHAT THE PIPE MIGHT DO; THE YOUNG LAWYER GESTICULATED TO OBSCURE PURPOSE; THIS SURELY WAS THE FOUNTAIN MADE FAMOUS BY SYMBOLISM!; ANOTHER PEA-SOUP FOG GRIPPED THE CUTER STREETS OF FRISCO; SOMETHING UNSPEAKABLE OOZED FROM THE BLOATED OBJECT; "MY CARD, SIR," THE EGREGIOUS SNOB TITTERED HANDSOMELY; IT WAS SOON OBVIOUS THAT KALENKOV'S FLY WAS OPEN; "A PENNY SAVED," THE MURDERER LAUGHED COLDLY; THE CASINO HAD EMPTIED TO GAPE VULGARLY AT HER ANTICS; RAOUL HAD INJURED HIS ARM UNDER THE BIG TOP; WAS IT TO BE ANOTHER NIGHT OF DOMINOES?; "CORPORAL HITLER AT YOUR SERVICE!" THE PALE YOUTH BARKED IN PERFECT GERMAN; SOME OF THE PHOTOGRAPHS WERE DELIGHTFULLY SALACIOUS; BARBARA FRIETCHIE'S HOUSE, OLD GLORY PROUDLY ERECT; THE REAL REPORT WAS, OF COURSE, ON THE BOTTOM; MYRNA FELT LIKE UNDRESSING FOR THE CONDUCTOR; DESPER-ATELY, HE COMPUTED THE DISTANCE TO SCRANTON; WHY DID THE FRUITERER KEEP LOOKING IN THE KITCHEN WINDOW?; COUNTRY BUMPKINS AT "HOT FEET," A FAVORITE PASTIME; THE WHISKEY HAD FINALLY DONE ITS UNHOLY WORK; FOR SOME REASON, ALEX FOUND HIMSELF LEANING ON THE DESK; THEY MADE A SINISTER DUO, ALL RIGHT; HIS HANDS SHOOK ON THE PRICELESS ARBALEST; THE MOB DEMANDED A HANDICAPPED

PORNO-FILM INSTEAD; "THE SPAM ROAST LOOKS GOOD TO ME," THE CONVICT LIED; THE BANKER PUSHED A PILE OF GOLD FLORINS TOWARD THE SHAMEFACED MATRON; PERHAPS THIS NOVEL WOULD GAIN DOYLE THE RESPECT HE CRAVED; "FUCK YOU, ME HEARTY!" THE PARROT RASPED; THE COUNTRYSIDE WAS AS TAXONOMIC AS EVER; THE PERVERT SAT PERFECTLY STILL IN THE LOCKER; SOON PROFESSOR MOKO WOULD BE ON THE RED BALL EXPRESS; THE SNOB ARROGANTLY READ THE LABEL; NIGHT FELL AWKWARDLY ON THE LAKE COUNTRY LEECHES; YET UNDER-NEATH HIS DINNER CLOTHES, SENATOR WEEP FELT BEAUTIFUL!; BLUE METAL SCARP; POSTSTRUCTURALISM HAD WORKED ITS INHUMAN SPELL AGAIN; PEPE DROPPED THE BATHROOM KEY INTO THE POISONED WELL; THE SPOILED PRIEST KNEW NOTHING OF COUTURE; COOLLY, WILLIS TOOK AIM AT THE TRIO OF GAMBOL-ING MAIDENS; BUT WHAT WAS THAT BENEATH THE BENCH?; HE HID, BITTERLY ASHAMED OF HIS OUTRÉ PLUS FOURS; HE LOOKED TO BE ANOTHER UNWANTED PROFESSOR COME TO CALL; "IT'S ALL GREEK TO ME," URSULA GRUNTED SUGGESTIVELY; THE STARS WERE, AS USUAL, PRETENDING LIFE.

Owns closes the book and places it on Chainville's desk amid a distracting collection of useless artifacts and bric-a-brac of an irritating preciosity. Lighting a cigarette, he laughs theatrically and, turning to a lamp, remarks, "Well, Cassandra, my dear, it seems that you were wrong. But surely, it's not, ha ha ha, as serious as all that, is it now?" He kicks the desk chair against the wall and then brings down every curse he can think of on the heads of all women: living, dead, and as yet unborn.

⮞ VIEW ⮜

Here is another view, taken from a different angle, of Olga Chervonen's country house. The field and trees behind it are barren, and the snow seems especially white in the winter sunset. It has occurred to many commentators and local historians that Madame Chervonen's house has never been seen by anyone in any season other than winter, and all the photographs, in this group at least, show the house "in the grip of icy fingers," as the late Bart Ballesteros once carelessly remarked. Of course, there may be many more photographs of the house, revealing it amid the splendors of other, more benign seasons, but nobody has ever come across them.

There is a chimney, and so on. A door, windows.

Inside the house, there are what those of a precise turn of mind might term clear indications of the absence of Madame Chervonen. She has, indeed, been dead for many years, but the photograph is undated, and so a good deal of uncertainty prevails. As is usually the case. Who was it said that photographs always lie? Or is that quite what was said? And when precisely was it, whatever it was, said?

After a time, the quarrel between Isidor Martin and Claude Urbane concerning the mysterious letter had become so heated and confused that no one seemed to remember very much of it, except for Madame Chervonen, who was only too maliciously happy to reprise the contretemps in its most minute details. No one, however, can now recall them. Martin and Urbane are also dead, and the official records attest that they are buried in separate plots, despite their being twins for many years. It is clear that the long bitter night was a snowy one, and that, in the morning, the letter had somehow been forgotten, perhaps mercifully.

Recently, an article in a small weekly newspaper mentioned Louis Bill's knowledge of certain events of that night and the following day, and reported that Bill was hesitant to speak of them. Claudia Bedu, Mr. Bill's companion for many years, insisted that he had never known Madame Chervonen or any of her circle, so-called, and that he worked hard for a living as a specialty dyer. "Baloney!" those in the know, or swim, protested.

❧ DREAMS ❧

Marcus Tommie took to dozing at his desk throughout the long, desperate afternoons. He sat straight in his chair, his head slightly bent so that the ruthless overhead lights created a glare on the lenses of his spectacles, thus concealing his closed eyes from the clerks who sat hopelessly at their desks in rows before him. His hands were invariably frozen in divers meaningless attitudes of crushingly boring office work; that is, they were stilled in one of the positions of what appeared to be the time-honored and occasionally useful process of selecting certain of the papers on the desk, so that these might then be addressed or confronted in one clerical fashion or another. Read, perhaps, or puzzled over. Thought about, annotated. Signed. *Acted upon!* It was somewhat surprising, even to the more jaded employees of Ballesteros Drain and Faucet's Contract-Rider Reinvigoration Department, over which Mr. Tommie presided, that he could keep so still for so long a time. His head was motionless, as were his arms and hands. He breathed quietly and evenly. His bald spot seemed to take on an aspect of judicious, if somewhat ludic authority, pointed, as it was, toward his subordinates.

Contemporary newspaper accounts, along with certain— supposedly mislaid—professional studies rumored to be, at the very least, alarming, conjecture that Mr. Tommie did not actually *dream* during these mensomastatic periods, but that words, singly or in combination, would come to him, and conjure up not the objects and concepts toward which they, as usual, rather pathetically gestured, but ideas of *other* objects, *other* concepts, *other*, if it is not too much to claim, realities. Mr. Tommie's eyes would flutter sightlessly open as he discerned in the murk of his unconscious such combinatories as "color of pure heads," "terminal breasts of the human garment," "transparent whiteness of delicate blue-metal glass," "fabric bathroom slides easily," etc., etc. The foregoing are, of necessity, officially invented samples intended merely to suggest the sort of substitutions to which Mr. Tommie was subject. What *other realities* such phrases created are lost or closed to the public, or whatever passes for it. "Dreamers," or so respected scientists say.

It might be well to remember that Proust had much the same experiences as Mr. Tommie, although the two had never heard of each other. The maestro writes, apropos of speaking in a dream: " 'But you know quite well I shall always live by her side, dear, deer, deer, Francis Jammes, fork.' . . . If I still repeated: 'Francis Jammes, deer, deer,' the sequence of these words no longer afforded me the limpid meaning and logic which they had expressed for me only a moment before, and which I could not now recall. I could not even understand why the word 'Aias' which my father had said to me just now had immediately signified: 'Take care you don't catch cold,' without any possibility of doubt." Proust notes that this process ceases to operate "on the surface where the world of the living opens."

These dream words of Mr. Tommie's had unexpected effects on him. On one occasion, he fell to the floor, weeping, and attempted to cover his bald spot with his least memorable tie; on another, he made objectionable and harassing remarks concerning secondary cigarette smoke, the delights of housework, and plastic tampon-applicators to a young file clerk busy with her daily manicure; and on yet another, he called loudly for the painful death of his dead father, whom he apostrophized as Mr. Packard, and who, he swore, lived in one of his desk drawers so as to haunt him.

So his long career as a lower-level executive proceeded rather uneventfully, but for the fashions, of course, the ever-changing fashions! Witnesses have also spoken of the always and unnecessarily different dust jackets on the book which lay, a permanent object of sorts, just to the left of his pristine desk blotter. He is, happily, dead at last, they say.

⫷ SENTENCE ⫸

When Yolanda Philippo boarded the train, the thought, which she was certain would come to her, did, indeed, come to her. Perhaps it is too much to call it a thought, since it was but a sentence. Her vocation as an art critic, however, prevented her from considering the sentence as a message, for in her mind's eye—a phrase she particularly admired—she saw the sentence as if inscribed on a blank field. She saw, that is, not the message, but a drawing, a picture, of the message, a picture which represented the sentence, "Myrna felt like undressing for the conductor." Simple enough, and yet, Miss Philippo later thought, fraught, sublimely fraught, with mystery.

She was notably chic in a charcoal-grey tweed polo coat with a black Persian-lamb shawl collar, a navy-blue suit, sheer off-black stockings, and black suede pumps. On her shiningly coiffed head, she wore a small black hat with a dotted half-veil, and on her hands, black kid gloves. A letter, discovered in the archive of a contemporary, notes, not without levity: "Had Yolanda been Myrna, she would have had a good deal of undressing to *do!*"

Miss Philippo invariably had this thought, or, more accurately, saw this drawing, whenever she boarded a train, or whenever she thought of a train, or whenever she thought of people she knew who had, for private reasons, boarded trains. She also saw the drawing whenever she undressed or watched other women undress—not, her biographer asserts, a predilection—or thought of undressing. But who, or what, did "Myrna" signify?

Miss Philippo sat at the window, looking out on a frozen suburban scene whose delineations were thought interesting to novelists of a certain bent. There were the icicles hanging from the eaves! There was a snowman! And so on. The conductor arrived at her seat, and as she watched him punch her ticket, she thought how much she felt like undressing for him, despite his essential repulsiveness. Yet she was *not* Myrna, as she well knew.

Many years earlier, when Miss Philippo had been a graduate student, a professor with sexual designs on her took her to dinner at a newly fashionable restaurant in a newly fashionable neighborhood. Miss Philippo, exhausted, even before the entrée, medaillons de veau en robes blanches, by her battle with the professor's hot and importunate hands, excused herself and fled to the ladies' room. It was empty, save for one woman, some twenty years her senior, possessed of a beautiful, almost noble face, the face of Lesbia or Sulpicia. She leaned drunkenly against one of the black porcelain sinks, stripped to the waist, washing her bosom and crying uncontrollably into her reflection. Miss Philippo stood, embarrassed, then washed her hands at the sink farthest from the woman, whose full, heavy breasts were covered with purple bruises and teeth marks. It was, to the younger woman, an acute picture of despair.

This woman could have been the "Myrna" of Miss Philippo's repetitive sentence, although it is impossible to know why, and, surely, even more impossible to determine why such a "Myrna" would have had anything to do with trains or conductors. Whatever the solution to these puzzles, if they may so be termed, Yolanda Philippo contrived to imagine herself undressing for this repulsive conductor. He would bite her breasts, too hard, his stupid hat askew on his balding head.

Perhaps she dreamed it, and in her dream found herself seeing, *in her mind's eye,* the intransigent drawing, "Myrna felt like undressing for the conductor," released, free, wholly removed from all meaning, much like the wintry sunset which inhabited the sky as she emerged from the station.

⇒ MAPS ⇐

Balloons sent aloft, bearing messages that called Bill Juillard's sanity into question, became a commonplace during one period, and he bore this indignity fairly well. These incidents occurred after he had drawn the first representation, or, as it was popularly known, sketch of the tree whose inexorable path everything in his life was constrained to follow, and discovered, to his embarrassment, that no one could recognize the sketch as representative of a tree. Some looked at the drawing and laughed nervously, others stared at it stupidly (ice cream, as often as not, running down their forearms), a few stepped back, smartly, in disgust or fear, and many gasped and regarded the sketch with something approaching awe. But whatever the viewers did, and whatever they said, none ever took the *something* on paper for the image of a tree.

There were the inevitable idle onlookers, ne'er-do-wells, bums, loafers, and layabouts who wondered—loudly, for the media—why Juillard "bothers to show the goddamned thing at all!" And, sporadically, the infamous balloons were launched, bearing their sullen and disheartening messages. After a time, Juillard ceased all social activities, heeding his estranged wife's advice as delivered to him on a picture postcard of *Backyards in Flatbush:* "Fuck them!"

He did not, however, falter in his attempts to draw the tree, and over a long period of time made hundreds, if not thousands of sketches, drawing one next to another, sometimes one directly atop another, and always on sheets of paper measuring some three-by-four feet. One evening, a few years after he had begun this project, he looked at the sheet of paper he had been working on and realized that its surface, covered to the edges with pencil, ink, and crayon marks of all colors, represented a map! He soon looked through the other drawings he'd completed and saw that all of them were maps. He had made, he slowly came to believe, and all unknowing, a set of maps that could well show him the way to that place at which his static and surely perverse love festered in death, that place at which he could find all the things that he'd forgotten.

He bought a perfectly designed and crafted calibrated mileage calculator, made by Streicher Benz Roehm Gesellschaft, and spent endless hours at his table, rolling the instrument's little wheel back and forth over what were surely roads (surely they were roads!) on his invaluable maps. The past was waiting, somehow, in space.

Being a historian, he believed, of course, that the past is history, and that history, that which happened somewhere, can be retrieved, almost whole. But as the months and then the years passed, he revised, then doubted, and finally discarded these beliefs. The tortured scrawls on his stacks of paper, he came to know, were not the way to the past. They were the meaning of the past.

≫ MOTHER ≪

The woman was about to close the blinds against the bleak January day. She wore a plain black dress with a pleated skirt and soft white collar, and her bobbed black hair shone, even in the dim winter light. Her face was set in a rigid expression of anger and pain. She closed the blinds. This happened many years ago, as her clothing and hairstyle testified.

On the small, round table in the corner is a bouquet of flowers, tendered her two or three evenings ago by her husband, and a book. The book may be *American Beauty*, by Edna Ferber, for certain clues, so to speak, suggested this. It is pointless to rehearse them; all are agreed on the matter. The woman turned from the window, turns back, opens the blinds. She looked out, closes the blinds again, then switched on a lamp and began to unbutton her dress. She pushes it off her shoulders and down to her waist, slipped off the straps of her chemise and lets that, too, gather at her waist in a gleaming white cloud. She walked to the bathroom.

Now she stood before the mirror, soaping her arms, under-arms, shoulders, and breasts, watching the tears running down her face. She looks quickly toward the open door, and there was her three-year-old son, staring at her nakedness. She shook her head in patient exasperation. Holding one forearm across her soapy breasts, the woman grasped the collar of the boy's mackinaw, and quickly propels him toward the half-open kitchen door and out onto the wooden steps leading to the backyard. She steps inside, closes and locked the door, and returns to the bathroom. As she began to rinse herself, loud, rasping sobs broke forth from her, reverberant in the small space of the room. Curiously, the palms of her hands were pressed flat over her nipples.

The boy, wretched in the barren yard, frightened yet enrap-tured by the sight of his mother, a beautiful, overwhelming stranger, untied his shoelaces and returned to the kitchen door. It was locked, and he started to cry. He wants his mother to tie his shoelaces, to let him into the warm kitchen, to hold him against her mysterious flesh. Crying louder, he pushes at the kitchen door, and it suddenly opened. The kitchen was empty, and the boy walked to the bathroom. It, too, is empty, but redolent of perfumed soap. He calls wildly for his mother. There was no reply.

The woman is Claire Hounsfield, the wife of an adulterous banker, James Hounsfield. Little is known of him save that he has a great interest in and weakness for real-estate speculation. He dies penniless. Claire is still alive, but no one cares about this one way or another. Her son, Ivan, is a successful and charming university community-liaison officer with pronounced sociopathic tendencies.

⮞ PATIENTS ⮜

To the distress of Dr. Sydelle Lelgach, newly appointed chief of psychiatry at the Pelepzin Hospital, Jonathan Tancred calls the institution a "crackerjack factory." What is of more pressing concern to her, however, is that he has taught the other patients to do his joy-fire dance, an awkward, grotesque, agitated hopping from foot to foot, the eyes closed, the hands either in the pockets or on the hips. All the patients, save the infirm and crippled, do the dance during the daily exercise period, and the grounds are filled with shrieks of maniacal laughter. The attendants, but lately instructed in the negative aspects of brutality, a concept dear to their hearts, stand by, consumed with rage at the thought that the loonies may be enjoying themselves, even though their laughter is clearly devoid of pleasure.

Dr. Lelgach has had little success with Tancred, who answers her questions, when he answers them, in disjointed phrases, and invents grisly stories about three young women, sisters, who were, he says, characters in a book his mother used to read to him. He insists, or, as he puts it, he *knows* that the women were real, for they often stood below his window at night, their white dresses weirdly luminescent in the darkness. During their sessions, he continues to stare lewdly and brazenly at the doctor's legs, and when she changes position in her chair, tries to look up her skirt. Against her better judgment, she takes to wearing slacks on those days when she will be seeing Tancred —although, she bitterly acknowledges, he is the one who is seeing *her!* She despises herself for her weakness.

There is a kind of outbuilding on the edge of the grounds, used now for the storage of gardening equipment, but which once must have served as a caretaker's cottage. It is, in fact, known as the Cottage. There is a chimney, a door, windows, and so on. Whenever it snowed, the light glared off the white-piled roof, the brightness thereby effected disquietingly like that of California sunlight. Some of the maniacs scream that from time to time people are seen—people with "white faces"—looking out the windows at them. One day, after a particularly frenzied performance of the joy-fire dance, the cottage miraculously burst into flames. The hysterical celebration which ensued was put down with unusual force, considering the newly enlightened attitudes of the attendants. They had, or so it seemed, their orders.

Two weeks later, Tancred was transferred to the Sunset Haven Psychiatric Correctional Institute, a maximum-security teaching hospital. Dr. Lelgach was absent on the day of the transfer, putatively suffering from an intestinal viral infection. When she returns, she finds a note, written in black crayon, on her desk. Its contents make her feel nauseous and unaccountably vile:

Dear Doc.,
  Don't you know that I can see the filthy EVIDENCE right through your doctor costume?
                              Cordially,
                              J. Tancred

❧ SCULPTOR ❦

It is difficult to believe that this ruin of a man, sprawled in a chair, his back against the filthy wall of a derelict saloon, is the great sculptor Archibald Fuxer. His legs are leaden, his left arm hangs lifeless, his right arm rests on the scarred, sticky table, its hand clutching a glass of white port. His eyes, eyes reflecting near-paralysis, are dry and blank. That the brain which conceived of the dangerous but mysteriously serene "White Figures" series should shatter itself with alcohol is one of the enigmas of the artistic personality, the illumination of which permits us to understand nothing.

The summer at the lake had been wonderful so far, and Archie hardly missed his father, although he knew that his mother's and his aunt's silences and glances at each other meant something. Things were awry, a word he had read and understood, more or less. But there was swimming, rowing, walks, picnics, visits to town and the lavish displays of *things* in Woolworth's. He put his hand into the water and the minnows disappeared in thin streaks of silver, then he splashed his face. Some leaves fell, those landing on the water scudding away in the delicious breeze.

He heard laughter, looked down along the shore from where he stood knee-deep in the shallows, and saw his mother and the grown daughter of the old couple who lived a short distance away from the summer cottages. They were lying on the picnic blanket, and his mother had her face inside the girl's open blouse and one of her legs thrown over her hips. The girl's blouse had fallen off her shoulders and his mother fondled and kissed her small breasts. The girl's hand was inside his mother's white shorts. Fear battered him, and, numb, he took a step toward the bank to hide, to fall into the wet mulch of rotted leaves, to disappear, to die. As he crouched, he saw a gleam from a point some ten yards or so beyond his mother and the girl, and as he looked, he realized that it was the white bathing suit of his aunt. She was watching his mother and the girl, perfectly still but for her right hand, which she moved slowly between her thighs. Archie watched them all and when his eyes began to burn he sat hunched in the ooze, distraught and in turmoil and sickeningly excited, until his mother and his aunt, their voices concerned but not yet worried, began to call him to come and help pack up. It was getting late.

He started toward them, whistling wildly and idiotically, slashing at the foliage with a switch. He called out, loudly, to his mother, who slowly shook her head, smiling, and waved at him. She was stunningly beautiful, as were the girl and his aunt, his lovely aunt. He felt as though he would weep, as though his belly would slide out of his body through his crotch. They were overwhelming. They were goddesses. They were the law.

Fuxer's disintegrated talents had little to do with these events of his eleventh year, or it may be that they were intimately connected to them. Alcohol, in any event, wrecked his brain. It is probable that months passed together when he completely forgot that summer. His mother has been dead for twenty years, his aunt for six, and the girl long ago disappeared into her life. He leans against the wall, bereft of the power of speech, looking, as Jules Renard wrote of Verlaine, like a drunken god, his head in the process of demolition. He stares ahead, his eyes burning.

⤷ ACCIDENTS ⤶

Here is one of the letters written by Joshua Bex, the celebrities' chemist. He lived amid the suffocating velvets and bibelots of pseudo-Victorian furnishings, which he called, perhaps in jest, "organic rubbish." He testified, at times loudly, that it soothed him, although there were widespread doubts. Behind a closed door of thick blue steel next to the cluttered mantel was the laboratory wherein the professor conducted a myriad of useless if flamboyant experiments, many of which had been scrupulously catalogued by clever boulevardiers, all now, fortunately, dead. He was, certainly, shunned by those who *really* mattered, but seemed oblivious to this. No one, of course, can ever peer into a heart, so the old songs maintain. Despite all, the work went forward. Excelsior! Bex muttered, when his stomach wasn't bothering him.

On this particular evening, he stood leaning on his desk, pressing down upon an addressed envelope with what looked like a spool, although blurred photographs of this by-now famous act have been used to prove otherwise; that is, the implement may have been a rubber stamp bearing a succinct message concerning human nature in all its intolerable manifestations, or it may have been a teleuton seal. Professor Bex heatedly claimed, so inquiries revealed, a family crest, which his colleagues, when sober, pretended to take seriously. A candle burned, quite unnecessarily, next to the green desk blotter, yet another beloved affectation.

Dear Son,

You did not fall down the stairs and smash your eye, although I understand that you profoundly wish this event, which never was, to be part of your life, your truth: you wish to incorporate this fantasy accident into the maelstrom of your childhood, into what Freud calls, if I am not mistaken, the "stupid creations" that invent us. You even "remember" the fall, the banister, the sharp pain as you struck the edge of the little table on the landing. But this did not happen. And may God forgive you, you certainly were not pushed down the stairs by your mother! You fell while on the way *upstairs*, and this had to do with the drunkenness of your grandparents, who scared you. Your mother, too, was drunk, but she was an innocent bystander, as they say. You were badly frightened, your grandmother had shouted at you to get to bed, you ran toward the stairs, tripped, and hit your cheekbone and eye on a step, exactly where the riser meets the tread. Nobody knew, for some time, that you'd lost the sight of that eye. I was working long hours then, and your mother, well, your mother was somewhat busy—you may recall her splendid salad-dressing displays and Worcestershire-sauce constructs, as well as the time she spent at the bathroom mirror, staring into her eyes while she washed herself, over and over.

As for the reference to the zeppelin, I know how angry you were about the disposition of that gift, but the sharp fin of that stupidly dangerous toy cut your anus quite badly. The doctor attended to you swiftly, of course, and you had more or less forgotten about the stitches when the first symptoms of your blindness began to manifest themselves. It was a harsh winter, in many ways.

My old lab was not precisely *seized* by the county, although your mother wanted you to believe that—furthermore, she didn't even want you to meet Emilia, my second wife. She was quite adamant about it, and never, *never*, I'm sure, missed an opportunity to denigrate and insult the ancient art of juggling when you were within hearing.

That's all I can really tell you about your accidents. I know that my memories were not your mother's, but she is dead now, and the truth will slowly out. Disguised and deformed as it may be, it's better than total fabrication. Probably.

love,
Father

While Professor Bex was posting the letter he had sealed earlier that evening—which may well be the letter (or a version of it) to which some have, by now, been made privy—the heavy laboratory door was somehow blown off its hinges by a concentrated explosion, allowing the curious, had any been about, to examine the smoldering remains of the professor's workroom rather carefully. There was, however, nothing of interest to be seen.

⮞ TWINS ⮜

Claude Urbane, the polo player, and his twin brother, Isidore Martin, a biologist of some local repute, were standing before their huge cheval glass, in order, as Urbane had said on certain splendid occasions in the past, "to see into the mirrored mirrors of the eternal comedy." This moment of mutual glass-gazing occurred some years before the sudden appearance, or apparition, of the famous snowman, about which much has been subsequently written.

Mirrors, so the brothers believed, tell us many things, although neither had ever satisfactorily explained what he meant by *things*. When pressed by journalists and attorneys, they invariably busied themselves about their small, tastefully furnished—save for the grotesque cheval glass—apartment. There always seemed to be something to do, considering the number of dirty vases and crusted egg cups situated in unlikely places.

Claude and Isidore, according to one particularly botched account, were seen from behind, and their faces were, of needs, reflected in the glass for the delectation and amusement of, so to speak, the cognoscenti, as well as many of the others.

Claude, of average height, slim, and wearing a corduroy Norfolk jacket and matching trousers of dark grey, carried a soft felt hat in his left hand, which was propped awkwardly upon his trunk in the vicinity of what Isidore knew to be a kidney. Claude's reflection was spoiled by his vapid grin, by now grown so familiar to his loved ones as to pass largely unremarked. Fellow chukkermen, however, often complained of its deleterious effect on their pony strings, or "pods." (It may be of importance to record that his jacket and trousers were, when worn together, sometimes called a Norfolk suit.)

Isidore, who stood next his brother, as might well be guessed, displayed all the characteristics of dwarfism, and was considered by numerous medical committees actually to *be* a dwarf. His reflected visage displayed a rueful mock chagrin. His left hand was placed, pronate, in what we know now to be a pathetic attempt at comedy, on his head, as if to say, "Look how small I am next to *you*, Claude!" Prosecutors have argued, to no avail, that Claude's imbecile smile had to do with Isidore's gesture. Isidore's suit was almost blatantly tiny, and his hat a misshapen horror, made even more reprehensible in comparison to Claude's dashing trilby, now, tragically, at the bottom of Dark Lake.

A feature story of the time in the Art and Life section of the local newspaper reported that "Isidore has suspected for many years that he is dwarflike, and much smaller than sportsman Claude, a rangy, elegant man with a quick smile, who likes to spend his rare leisure moments relaxing in his Norfolk outfit (which he good-naturedly calls a suit) and rakish trilby, a kind of hat. He will often burst into laughter, his eyes restlessly moving about the din [*sic*]."

At the time of the snowman's appearance, or apparition, many of Olga Chervonen's guests were surprised to see Claude and Isidore arrive at the great dancer's house, their size disparity even more cruelly in evidence because of the smaller brother's long absence from society, so-called. When Edward Carmichael bitterly suggested that everybody try on everybody else's clothes and take turns looking through the blinds at the bleak January day, a difficult silence fell on the company, as all eyes focused on Isidore, who was about to place his left hand on his head in ritual self-loathing. A cry of "hot spinach!" from the kitchen broke the tension.

Olga's little black dress with its soft white collar was torn in the grim rush for victuals, yet she was coolly serene. That was, as may be conjectured, before Isidore noticed the snowman!

⋙ DRAWING ⋘

Joshua Bex is said to have once owned an early drawing by
Archibald Fuxer, one which the aging sculptor termed, in scattered moments of clarity, a study. It is generally agreed that it is
not the sort of drawing that the artist would be expected to
make, assuming that Fuxer ever drew at all, nor is it the sort of
item that Joshua Bex would be expected to care about, much
less be in possession of, endlessly busy, as he was, in the laboratory, with corrosive elliptics, aromatic cycloidals, inverted
mordent (pralltriller) lipsticks, and moray plungers. The drawing has dropped out of sight, and rumors concerning its imagery
attest to the probability that the scene which it depicts has been
somewhat altered since its creation. With this in mind, Emilia
Sladky, Bex's recently spurned wife, has circulated a question-
naire intended to locate the drawing, although why any ques-
tionnaire, however scrupulously answered, should act as a key
to ascertaining the whereabouts of the drawing is a mystery. (It
should be made clear that Bex was not made aware of this action
of Miss Sladky's, and given the perhaps absurd secrecy with
which the list of questions has been passed from noted celebrity
to noted celebrity, he may remain permanently unaware.)

Although the man's upper garment is a jerkin, tabard, weskit,
smock, or surplice, why is his lower garment a pair of faded
jeans?

Is the man the boy's father?

Is the boy a boy or a girl?

If a girl, is the man the girl's father?

Is the object on the boy's (or girl's) head a rubber ball or an
apple?

Is the instrument depicted an arbalest?

What of the plume on the hat?

If this is Archibald Fuxer's work, why is it signed with a
device which looks much like a partially completed and hastily

scribbled over tic-tac-toe game?

Does the plumed hat belong to the man or to the boy (or girl)?

Why does the man wear, around his waist, an early model of the corrosive elliptic?

What does this fashion tell us about the man?

Given the apparent heights of the man (5 feet, 9½ inches), boy (or girl) (4 feet 11 inches), and pole (27 feet, 6 inches), how did the plumed hat arrive atop the pole?

Why are the two spectral trees in the background white (as dresses, as clouds (?) of underclothes, as handkerchiefs)?

At what or whom does the man aim the instrument?

Is the man a man or a woman?

If the latter, does this explain the otherwise disturbing presence of the corrosive elliptic (early model)?

What do Isaac and Iphigenia have to do with this *ersatz* pastoral?

If the man is a woman, is she the boy's (or girl's) mother?

Since the boy (or girl) partially obscures the pole so that the eye cannot follow its form, unbroken and uninterrupted, from its higher end (which sports the plumed hat) to its lower (which is sunk, to an indeterminate depth, into the ground), is it possible that there are two poles, the higher of which does not support the plumed hat, but rather depends from it?

If this latter is the case, may the phenomenon fairly be called a miracle?

In the light of Fuxer's mature work, especially the "White Figures" series, the "Gynophobia" group, and the "Harlow Warbucks" similitudes, can the two spectral white trees' absent color be considered fuchsia?

If the instrument is not an arbalest, it is a moray plunger?

Why does Yolanda Philippo, for one, think of the forest glade in which the two figures stand as a barren, cold backyard?

Can the face of a forest sprite (or fairy) be discovered amid the leaves?

Are the boy's (or girl's) eyes closed, or is such an appearance but a flaw of draftsmanship?

Where, in the (probably) pre-altered drawing was the kitchen sink located?

Was the kitchen sink subsequently substituted for by the arbalest (or moray plunger)?

Does this (possible) substitution explain the curious shadows?

Has the man (or woman) employed a technique known jocularly as "Kentucky windage"?

What clues indicate that the man (or woman) has recently been wading?

Do the figures seem to be in the process of demolition?

If the instrument depicted is, indeed, an arbalest, does it show any signs of lately being pulled from the waters of a dark lake?

What subtly different signs of such immersion would a moray plunger reveal?

Does the drawing indicate its having been kept in some sort of blue metal container?

What does professional-celebrity intuition proclaim the likely reason for the plumed hat's (seeming) perch atop the (a) pole?

Are the two spectral white trees as spectral and as white as the unique snowman?

If these two trees' absent color can be considered fuchsia, what then is the path of the signifier?

If there are legitimate clues which will help in answering any (or all) of these questions, why do they, inexplicably, point everywhere at once?

⇒ HALL ⇐

The hall is stifling. On the dais, Claude Luxo, the fireworks king and presiding chairman, is standing and furiously ringing a bell to quiet the maddened, quarreling, screaming crowd of zoning delegates, real-estate agents, their substitutes and proxies, lobbyists, guests, onlookers, and paid provocateurs. Luxo's three deputies, the bankers James Hounsfield and John Cerjet, and Sheldon Marius, the feminist draftsman, sit in silent awe and growing fear as the seething mass of sweating, enraged members of the housing delegations curse and shout themselves hoarse, all of them in total disregard of the wildly clanging bell.

"There is a louvered shutter on either side of a closed window!"

"The frame is painted white—"

"—as are the shutters! The house into whose wall this window is set is, apparently, an *old one.*"

"In the COUNTRY?"

"Or the suburbs?"

"The house may possibly be in *the city!*"

"The house is . . . whitewashed?"

"There is a low stone or granite wall running alongside the house . . ."

"And between it and the house there is a straggly, rather pathetic tree."

"Or SHRUB!"

"It might be a sumac, an ailanthus, or a cotoneaster!"

"Slowly falling, falling, and at the *same angle,* are eight leaves."

"Sere?"

"And of a uniform . . . brown . . . in color?"

"They're from *another* tree!"

"A DIFFERENT tree!"

"One which does not grow on *this* property!"

"Behind the window, three sisters—"

"—dress for Mass. Their names are . . . are . . . unknown."

"Their ages, too, are unknown, their physical characteristics . . . ?"

"Also UNKNOWN!"

"Grrrr!"

"Two of them are in white dresses."

"And the other?"

"Is in the process of sliding *her* white dress on over a . . . white
slip."

"One of the sisters looks out a window on the other side of
the room and remarks on . . . remarks on . . . on . . . on . . . the . . ."

"On the . . . the . . . BEAUTY of the dark lake which they have
always thought of as *theirs!*"

"The presence of this lake proves—"

"—beyond fear of contradiction—"

"—more or less—"

"—that the house is, indeed, in the COUNTRY!"

"Now the sisters are ready, and leave the room."

"White, lacy handkerchiefs are pinned so as to cover their . . .
their . . ."

"HAIR!"

"Each carries a Missal!"

"A missile?"

"A MISSAL! A MISSAL! MISSAL!"

"The door closes."

"There is a sudden . . . *penetrant* . . . *silence.*"

"Eight leaves fall."

"Slowly."

"All at the *same angle!*"

"One of the shutters bangs, in the sudden cold wind, against
the house."

"Oh GOD!"

Luxo continues to ring his bell frantically, an absurd and
pathetic figure amid the pandemonium of incensed housing
experts.

⇒ WAITER ⇐

After performing his duties at the Annual Feast with the lack of élan expected of him, Norman Bob was once again without funds, his salary and gratuities having been spent on gin, his favorite beverage, one which Bob referred to as the "blue banisher of images." He found another job to keep himself satisfactorily numbed, and was soon after spotted in the main dining room of a crowded restaurant, sharpening a carving knife before a large roast fowl. His Louis Bonaparte dress suit was becomingly stained and spotted with food and wine.

The restaurant, Le Chagrin, long since fallen into the dark waters of the lake, was distinguished not so much for its cuisine, which was barely adequate, but for its sullen, drunken waiters, hired specifically to give diners the sense of being harassed and insulted by lackeys far inferior to themselves. Such treatment tinged their many privileges with sweet guilt. The restaurant was also prized among the cognoscenti for its superb repetitive-expressionist paintings—vast grey canvases that dominated every wall and registered what Yolanda Philippo termed "post-gestural despair." Less sophisticated diners thought the paintings wall panels of a subtle delicacy.

The blue steel of Bob's knife reflected the somewhat harsh light of the dining room, his unwashed hair exuded a thin, scummy film of pomade, and his trousers, unbelted and un-braced, sagged over his battered, laceless shoes. The latter were a queasy yellow-brown, the color of decay, disease, shit, piss, paralysis, death, and the roast fowl.

Occasionally, guests would ask the waiters to empty their bladders on them, but reservations for such piquancies of dining had, understandably, to be made in advance. Operating records, luckily preserved when Le Chagrin disappeared, note that the odor of juniper, of which Bob's urine reeked, was espe-cially prized by the clientele. There was something particularly coarse and lasting about it. On this evening, however, Bob pulled a shriveled penis, barely visible between his greasy fingers, from his gaping fly, and, turning toward a table of diners, pissed on his own trousers and shoes.

From the dim, filthy kitchen, the chef, a woman dressed in a torn, soiled slip from whose tattered lace bodice one of her breasts partially protruded, looked delightedly at the table of diners, all of whom were enthusiastically applauding the sodden Bob's impromptu performance. In her always enthralling diary, she recorded: "At that moment, I really felt like undressing for the waiter."

⇛ OBSESSION ⇚

Some time ago, Sandor Skariofszky smashed his little barrel bank. He sits now for hours at his table, the retrieved coins mixed with a bagful of invaluable gold *reales*—sometimes known as *pendejos de oro*—piling and repiling the shining currency into small stacks, counting it, staring and bewildered. This behavior, which is inconsistent with Skariofszky's particular compulsion, began one afternoon, when, examining his imitation Hudson River painting in his usual intense way, he was seized by the desire to see the faces of the three young women wading in the lake, for he unexpectedly came to know that one of them represented his late mother, the Countess Skariofszky-Poniatowsky del Príncipe. Taking up his powerful magnifying glass, he studied the three white figures for days, sometimes not moving from the picture for hours together. Occasionally, he thought that he could make out facial features on one or more of the images, but such features, were they even present, were always, as it were, generic: any eye or any nose or any mouth. They were, in effect, the features that indifferently compose the faces of snowmen. At other times, stare as he might, he could discern *only* white dresses, or *only* pastel picture hats; and often, the figures asserted themselves as rays of light falling through the dense tree canopy onto the tranquil surface of the water. His spirits invariably sank to their lowest ebb when all that he could identify for certain were three determined strokes of cadmium white.

There was no one to whom he could talk about this, for Old Tony had moved to another city and a new life as part-owner of a meatless luncheonette, the Sans-Which Shop. Skariofszky's obsession—for that is what the yearning to see the girls' faces had become—was not tempered or abated by any activity what-soever. He had lost all interest in envelopes, in dancing, in the writing of obsequious letters to famous yet touchingly ordinary film stars; and he avoided all games of chance, even Old Auntie's Solitaire. Most indicative, perhaps, of the gloom and apathy into which he had sunk, he paid no more attention to his wardrobe and let his adored mouth go wrong. He had, of course, stopped saving coins, since that process had been entirely part of the old satisfyingly compulsive ritual. Now he but sits, as noted, at the table, playing with his coins, his stunned face vague and stupid.

Yet in the past week an idea has come to him, one which has begun to fill him with hope. It is a simple idea, and like so many simple ideas, wholly maniacal: Skariofszky has the idea of reproducing the painting to the *actual scale* of the depicted scene. He will, certainly, need much more money than he presently has in order to find and then buy the vast tracts of land on which the painting can be replicated, but he can always return to the concert stage, despite his crippled embouchure. Then, too, he will have to engage Robert Bedu, who may be able to find some way around the almost insurmountable problem of moving the tons of canvas needed to cover some five hundred square miles of ground.

But if he can raise the money, and if Bedu—or somebody—is interested and available, and if he can come to a financial agreement with the contractors necessary to such a project, the three girls will absolutely emerge as life-sized figures, their faces clear, their mouths eager to speak. Skariofszky envisions himself splashing through the water of the huge canvas lake toward the young women, who are about to turn, to reveal themselves! But as he gets closer, his arms stretched toward them, they look like, they seem to be rays of light falling through the leaves of the giant trees, three enormous impasto strokes of cadmium white.

⋙ COLLEAGUES ⋘

Robert Bedu, the inventor of the Symptomatic Referent Equalizer, a disarmingly simple microchip search-functional dublend, was seated at his desk, his head propped wearily on his left hand, his right hand slowly pushing his heirloom fountain pen across a sheet of thick stationery. Alert observers, or so their reports maintained, noted that the stationery was 65 percent rag and that the pen, a heavy, gold-nibbed masterpiece of tortoise shell, was a rare Baron-Canterel. Bedu was writing a letter to Louis Bill, a tool-and-die maker, his old colleague from that time the professional newsletters like to call—with, admittedly, a touch of the maudlin—their "garage days." There certainly were a lot of memories, as many of their contemporaries could easily imagine. Bedu, patiently and unenthusiastically, guided his pen across the creamy writing paper, made to his specifications somewhere in Europe, perhaps Switzerland. Bill would surely have known of the location of the "somewhere," although there is a chance that he would have been as much in the dark as Bedu's wife and family were. There was, as the phrase has it, no love lost between the two men, youthful collaborations notwithstanding. Bedu's hand was growing weary. For that matter, both his hands were tingling, almost, as it is said, asleep. Perhaps he laughed to himself at the truism that notoriety and fame in the chip world, or, as sophisticates said, the World of Chips, did not preclude fatigue. He stopped writing, capped his pen, and read the letter.

Dear Louis:

I've been having a recurring dream lately. In it, you pound at the door to my kitchen, wherein I'm preparing what seems to be a large Greek salad in the sink. This strikes you as funny and you open a very ugly suitcase to show me that it contains the stolen prototype of the Symptomatic Referent Equalizer. At this point, the dream ends and I wake up hating you as I hated you years ago, when your ingenuousness, so-called, cost me my fiancée, my university chair, and my country house. It was never, as you surely know, my fault that you and Madame Chervonen exchanged confidences during those long, snow-bound nights while the others slept, played cards, or drank themselves insensible. Yet you blamed me and took your revenge. I suppose I'm trying to say that your slanderous story of the revelatory letter started everything. I hope that you were at least *occasionally* happy with Claudia, another dupe of the letter's snide implications. So you see that I have not grown utterly indifferent to compassion even where you are concerned. Claudia also appears in my dream, smiling that faithless smile we both learned to dread.

To sum up my feelings—a crass phrase, I know. I despise you and will never forgive you. I am working very hard, with the aid of a para-psychologist and a new imaging technique called *graphosemiophonics*, to dream you into death.

I am, always,
Robert Bedu

☙ STAIRS ❧

Joshua Bex's letter to his son, Caleb, a moderately successful lawyer specializing in diminished-capacity suits, did nothing to dispel or dull the younger man's crystalline but perhaps spurious memory. It was this memory, such as it was, which possessed him, which had shaped his childhood, his adolescence, and his adulthood. To read his father's letter was intolerable, filled, as it was, with cravenly self-serving, transparently defensive lies about his mother's supposed innocence, her bitter unhappiness. She had been, Caleb *knew*, cruel and drunken and careless, a sloven reeking of alcohol and vomit and piss, moving amid a whiskey haze from within which she pushed him roughly away.

And one day she pushed him down the stairs. He still sees, with tortured lucidity, the small table on the landing growing fantastically larger as he hurtled toward it, his scream preceding him. On the table was a glossy black Chinese teapot around whose girth and spout coiled a red dragon; a photograph, in a busy silver-gilt frame, of his grandmother, regal in a fur coat and dark cloche, standing next to a gleaming Packard sedan; and a copy of *The Good Earth*. There was a crash. His head burst into flashes of light, and pain sliced heavily into his skull.

His mother's face, stunned and vacant, became clear for a moment. Then it disappeared into vaguely reddish darkness. He awoke, lying face down on the living room couch, naked below the waist. The doctor's finger was thrust all the way into his rectum.

"Poor boy!" "Oh my God!" "Oh dear!" "Poor boy!"

It doesn't matter what his father has to say, ever. Caleb *knows*. He is emotionally in stasis, caught in his weirdly plausible history. His life has arranged itself so as to make it impossible for him to come to terms with dozens of things—open fields, clumps of dark trees, freaks, the smell of tea, snow, juggling, sugar cookies, wind-up toys, women's hosiery, football, the sound of chickens clucking in the deadly heat of still summer afternoons, and many others. These things sometimes appall, sometimes attract, sometimes excite him. None of these responses is even momentarily free from the paralyzing anxiety that the things cause.

Caleb thinks, again, of his father's letter, which he knows by heart, or so he believes. It is, of course, the kind of letter that one might expect, after God knows how many years, from the discredited and disgraced charlatan, all of whose possessions, including his pathetic laboratory, were seized for nonpayment of taxes; from a weakling, married—illegally!—to a cheap carnival slut, a flat-chested tramp of a cunt whore with the talent of a monkey! Caleb mutters and scowls.

He turns a corner, scowling, his hands jammed into his overcoat pockets, a cigarillo between his thin lips, and his gaze is unexpectedly arrested as he strides past a parrot on a perch, a cup chained next to his filthy claws. The parrot looks at him and cocks his head.

"Poor boy!" the bird says. "Poor boy!"

Caleb scowls more darkly and crosses the street. In the briefcase tucked under his arm is a pistol. Perhaps today something ugly would die.

⇒ HORSES ⇐

Sir Evelyn Jenn and his slow-witted manservant, Lafcadio Bob, were out in the blustery autumnal fields, searching for evidence of the recent unwanted presence of swarthy gypsies. Sir Evelyn was mounted on Count Iago, a zany horse of oddly unbalanced features, and Lafcadio, as usual, led the animal by the bridle. It was difficult for Sir Evelyn to *consider*, so to speak, Count Iago, for invariably that made him remember that he was out of Queen's Cookie by Billy Sunday. "Darn!" he would say, and "Nuts!" in his terrifying old-boy whine, for Count Iago's sire always made him think of his ex-wife.

Solange McCarty, whom he married despite family objections to her name and incoherent background, was nineteen when he first stared at her, goggle-eyed, as she modeled lingerie and foundation garments "For the Young Career Woman" at one of the Jenntille showrooms: he was fifty-two. They were wed soon after, and some few years later were solidly *placed*, as an exciting couple, in the moneyed society of vague cruelties and dim conversation that Sir Evelyn had managed partially to avoid during his long bachelorhood. Solange had, by this time, become a famous clotheshorse, and their daughter, Ann, had been born, to plaudits and champagne.

Ann was soon the problem, of course, or, as Sir Evelyn often put it to the third-rate portraits of his ravaged ancestors, "The girl is one heck of a handful!" The sort of handful that she was said to be was never quite clarified, but there it apparently was! A handful. A clearer problem, however, was the manner in which the marriage began to cool rapidly, becoming little more than a distantly correct friendship, as soon as Solange, in what Sir Evelyn stupidly saw as a deferential attempt to please him, began seriously to address herself to an all-consuming equestrianism. Had Sir Evelyn been of a more suspicious turn of mind, or had he but spoken to Lafcadio—whose powers of observation had been thoroughly developed by his brother, Norman, the unofficial dean of waiters—he might have discovered what all the stable boys knew: that Ann's father was, quite probably, Billy Sunday.

There had been signs that Sir Evelyn had not seen, chosen not to see, or misinterpreted. Oats, for instance, seemed always to be caught in Solange's hair or the folds and pockets of her clothes; the faint odor of manure and apples clung to her underwear; she had, often, inexplicably symmetrical bruises on her inner thighs; she walked with slow and painful gait after each afternoon spent working in the stables; and so on. Most astonishingly, Sir Evelyn apparently accepted, without comment, the basketlike leather harness that Solange had specially made for her in Mexico, as an aid, she informed her admiring husband, to "treetop bird-watching."

Ann relentlessly grew into a scattered and, at times, utterly psychotic young woman. Solange, after the death of Billy Sunday, had a series of reckless affairs with grocery clerks, stockbrokers, pinboys, policemen, assistant professors, longshoremen, feminist politicians, and homosexual athletes, then divorced Sir Evelyn. The tycoon's empire grew larger and larger. For many years after the huge scandal in which Ann figured as an aggravating influence, he was content to pay all the bills for what he called—on the advice of his attorneys—her "European sojourn," and to send her sumptuously expensive jewelry and exquisitely gossamer Jenntille lingerie each Christmas and birthday. The nuns, of course, immediately seized and hid the gifts lest they excite her to what they spoke of as "the fever." Sister Harry Angelica thought that a peach teddy was some sort of dessert and wondered how long it would keep on ice. Such were the rare diversions in the convent.

The light was fading and the fields growing dim in the cold mist. The wind, more blustery with the onrush of twilight, drove directly into their faces as they headed for the house, a good fire, and, for the master, cognac and a half hour or so before his favorite painting, an anonymous daub of the Passaic

River school, "View of White Girls at Metal Lake." Lafcadio, whose mind had been lurching through fragments of the past, called up from near-oblivion by whatever chain of lunatic associations, looked up at Sir Evelyn and smiled happily.

"He's a good brother," he said, stroking Count Iago's muzzle. "Crazy like his sister, oh yes, but nice and good."

Sir Evelyn stared at him through the gloom and swirling mist. What the heck is the imbecile on about now? "Gosh, yes, right!" he said. Count Iago neighed distractedly.

⤳ SILENCE ⤴

The draftsman and illustrator who changed the entire conception of advertising graphics, and who, in his later years, was celebrated for his delicate, radically designed, and ambiguously captioned comic strip, *The Rebellious Bravo*, Hubert-Allen Zipp ("Haz"), began, for whatever reason, to think of his childhood; more precisely, thoughts of his childhood were thrust upon him. People remarked upon his bearded face set in a kind of pained repose, his eyes closed, "dead to the world," as a colleague put it, not knowing how correct the remark was.

Zipp thought, most often, of the small apartment in which, as a child, he had lived, with his mother, for three or four years. There seemed no particular reason for his mind to keep returning to this apartment, for it not only revealed nothing to him, it, on the contrary, conspired to obscure those other things seized upon by his memory as possibly important.

When Zipp focused on a specific object it became, in his memory—although memory, according to Zipp, was not quite the word—something *else*. This might have been understood as an instance of mnemonic metamorphosis but for the fact that it was not truly the object which became other, but the name of the object which changed, so that the new name forever supplanted the old, or, as Zipp must have thought of it in order to preserve his composure, the real name. The object remained the same in all particulars, but its name properly belonged to something else, some other thing or person or place or idea or process or action. With this new title stubbornly attached to it, the original object became immediately unrecognizable, no more than an undifferentiated lump; yet the new title did not evoke the object proper to *it*, but existed as a floating phrase. Zipp felt that he was losing his mind and came to dread the unwanted reflections, which were now part of his everyday life. His past had become a frightening sea of unfixable data.

He thought, for example—although that word barely begins to cover the experience—a Philco floor-model radio a daybed, a Chinese porcelain tea set a silk kimono, a silver-painted radiator fried potatoes, a Gold Dust Twins cardboard carton a kitchen sink, dim white figures in a dark picture naked breasts. Sometimes, the changes were truly unnerving, the new title having a weirdly correct but occulted relationship to the object title supplanted, as, for instance, when Zipp erased thin leather belt with pink two-way-stretch girdle.

The new names filled him with a profound anxiety; he felt that if he could understand the reasons why the objects evoked names—or, as he had begun to think of them, captions—which refused to denote, explain, or illuminate them, which, in fact, disintegrated them, he might then be able to understand the fearsome emptiness of his childhood as well as the subtly disfigured adult life to which it had so relentlessly led. But he could never understand, and his attempts led him to more convoluted experiences, as on the night when a couple of aspirins became pubic hair. One morning, staring at the closed lids of his eyes, he conceived of himself as absolutely nothing, and a great silence, which turned to death, enveloped him.

⇒ COINCIDENCE ⇐

The importunate professor who surreptitiously attempted to caress virtually all of Yolanda Philippo's charms when, years before, she suffered as a graduate student, is discovered one autumn afternoon at the teller's counter—or, as this institution terms it in suffocating pretentiousness, the *caisse*—of the small, discreet bank in which he maintains a private account. The professor, tritely rumpled in a ghastly tweed topcoat and worn bowler, is withdrawing funds sufficient to ensure a four-day weekend of, he hopes, reasonable debauchery with Myrna, one of his current unfortunate graduates. She is a young woman of nervously erratic intelligence, and is possessed of a thin, almost scrawny body that seems to tremble with—so the professor believes—sexual energy. He is officially, to any who might care to inquire, on his way to one of the innumerable symposia that are among the dreadful occupational hazards of academic life, or, as his wife writes it to an old and cruelly unsympathetic friend, "life."

Some mildly surprising items of information, useless in themselves, should here be recorded. Myrna is the daughter of the sobbing woman, her breasts savaged, encountered in the ladies' room by Yolanda Philippo on that long-ago night when she fought off, for a time, the professor's tireless advances. The woman's husband, a friendly and gregarious corporate attorney, deacon of his Methodist congregation, and devoted runner, is her sexual despot and torturer, and is also the incestuous partner of their two young daughters, the older of whom, Myrna, will be registering, about now, for her reserved room in an intimate bed-and-breakfast on the edge of a too perfect lake, complete with whitecaps kicked up by the cool breeze. The requisite conifers, canoes, bass, etc., are also present. The professor, an amorous naïf despite his years as a lecher, has reserved the room adjoining: he and Myrna will present themselves as loving father and daughter, a relationship so unconvincing that even the jaded desk clerk will blush in embarrassment for them. Their first night passes sans notable catastrophe—the professor convinces himself that he has been kind, imaginative, unselfish, and spectacularly virile; and Myrna is thankful that her fist, jammed firmly into her mouth, turned her sobs into what the professor considered uncontrollable, lascivious groaning. Perhaps because of the irony of their counterfeit relationship, Myrna, right after breakfast the next morning, washes down fifty-three Amytals with a plastic tumblerful of vodka. When the professor discovers her body, he faints, then calls the police; his ensuing adventures, not least of which are those that feature his wife, resemble certain incidents in many hazy art films, some of which have enduring if limited success in university towns.

Two more ironies may help to strengthen, or weaken, the pathetic integument of this quasi-academic interlude. The first is that the handsome and sadistic husband of Myrna's sobbing mother sat just across from the professor and Yolanda Philippo's table in the restaurant, his face fixed immovably in a horrible and brutal smile as he waited for his wife's return from the ladies' room, in which she had spent more than ten minutes! An offense designed to humiliate him, of course! and for which she will be corrected! The second irony: Yolanda Philippo happened to travel on the same train which carried the professor and the doomed Myrna to their aborted amours. Miss Philippo may well have *seen* the professor, and even thought of how exciting it might be to undress for him, not having recognized the old man as the crude skirt-lifter of two decades past.

There are a few loose ends to this occurrence, or these occurrences, but they make little sense, being no more than isolated and opaque phrases, unintelligibly strewn about and quite impervious to rational inquiry. Actually to discover their import would probably lead to more revelations of alarming coincidence, followed by incredulous laughter. Yet coincidence is, in essence, the basis of all human action and behavior. Who can believe—dare anyone believe—that the professor's name is J. Thomas Conductor?

➣ POISON ⋐

Here is a table on which rest a plate, a glass, a carafe almost full of an unidentifiable dark liquid, silverware, and an unrecognizable, near-shapeless object, which may be a loaf of bread, part of one, or a partly filled hot-water bottle. On a nearby sideboard stand a shiny, possibly chrome-plated bucket and a bowl of spheroids.

Sitting at the table, Bart Ballesteros, the wealthy rake and heir to the Ballesteros Drain and Faucet fortune, contemplates a small bottle. He has no idea, perhaps, of the bottle's contents, and the drawn expression on his face may testify to his awareness of the other diners, nothing more, who are glaring at him disapprovingly. This assumes that there *are other diners*, none of whom, from this vantage, are in evidence. He draws the bottle, which he holds at eye level, close to his face, as if to read the small print on the label, no small feat for him and his notoriously weak eyes, of which many a bawdy "brothel story" has been told. He soon notices the bowl of spheroids, and speaks.

"Something unaccountably sad happened to me some years ago on a wintry patio. I hear, even now, a woman's voice, although it is muffled, peacefully remote; as if projected through thickly falling snow; as if dead." The other diners, if present, are growing restive, but Ballesteros continues. "What is more desolate than empty chairs drawn up to a supper steadily growing colder? Than that isolated bottle of Worcestershire sauce? Than the limp salad? Oh!"

Ballesteros abruptly drinks off the contents of the bottle, discovering that the liquid, while faintly bitter and with a hint of the rancid, is far from unpleasant. The other diners, let us assume, are now quite beside themselves at this display of vulgarity, but Ballesteros is unmoved. He is, of course, as good as dead.

Certain of Ballesteros's sycophantic friends later insisted, at his memorial gathering (from, it should be confessed, their safe position behind the Swedish meatballs), that dear Bart's last thoughts were of the arts which his money had literally called into being, and of a remarkable sunset over Aspen, described by one as "pale oranges, and savage, pale ochres, dissolving into the palest lavenders and swaggering, albeit pale crimsons, not to mention the pale yellows." It was also made clear that Ballesteros was smitten by the art one sees everywhere around one, if, as he was heard to remark on more than one occasion, "one really looks." How his eyes would move in and out of focus as he waited for the inevitable laughter that followed such *mots!*

Ballesteros, incidentally, in his restaurant death throes, kicked the bowl of spheroids off the sideboard. Several rolled toward the probable diners, who reacted predictably. In the jaundiced light of the restaurant, the spheroids took on a certain disturbingly translucent quality, still talked about. Ballesteros's ex-wife, Cassandra, has contested his will, which leaves the bulk of his considerable estate to Jeanne Souze, or Sousa, a nurse who has garnered unimpeachable medical kudos, and Ström Owns, a hard-hitting journalistic fictioneer, who is beginning to make a small name for himself as an unblinkingly honest actualist.

"It's all just a colloquy of errors," Cassandra often remarks, at her attorney's advice. Family friends consider her a psychological cripple, at long last.

➣ SIGHT ❦

Dr. LeFlave can no longer bear to look at his telescope, and even on such a night as this, refuses to employ it, or, for that matter, to enter the room which it so dominates; this particular night, doubtless, would be ideal for such astronomy as the doctor practices, since the brilliance of the moon has stolen some of the trillion stars' luster, in a phenomenon reminiscent of that remarked by Sappho:

Ἄστερες μὲν ἀμφὶ κάλαν σελάνναν . . .

even though this moon is a crescent, whereas Sappho's is "full and lacquers / All the earth with brightness."

Dr. LeFlave, it may be conjectured, has avoided his astronomical avocation ever since the night he gazed, rapt, yet filled with carnal anguish, on the man and three young women at their amusements, their silent and strangely serene dalliance, in which each played, it now seems to him, an assigned role. That he knows that he really could not have *seen* this scenario —*on the moon!*—neither soothes nor comforts him. However the images had come about, they persisted in their fearsome clarity.

But most disturbingly, certain relationships have made themselves manifest to him despite his floundering efforts to suppress them by manic and hysterical attention to such trivialities as professional dissertation contests, domestic idiot-politics, and the credos of film stars. Nothing satisfactorily functioned to cloak that which he knew to be the truth: that the man—he was tempted to think "the man in the moon," although levity, in such situation, seemed wholly out of place—whom he had seen in his white linen suit and Borsalino, energetically thrusting himself into the sweet flesh of the woman, was his father.

Soon after this knowledge, which terrified him, he unexpectedly realized that one of the women wading in the cool shallows of the lake was his mother, and that she was almost the same age as his father, not, as the image had at first presented itself, a post-adolescent girl. Each time now that his mother's beautiful face swam into his memory, he saw in it an expression that he had never dreamed she could wear. Her smile was secret and lascivious, her eyes hooded, conspiratorial, knowing, as she watched his father plunge into her fainting companion. It was bitterly clear that she had acted as his father's procuress: it was she who had provided this girl.

Dr. LeFlave reached, of needs, perhaps, one final conclusion concerning the grotesque tableau, one to which logic inevitably led him. If his parents had both been in their mid-twenties on that afternoon, then all had occurred some five or six years after his birth. This was terrible to him, awful, for he felt, in some inexplicable way, implicated in and soiled by this corruption.

He never made out the faces of the other two women, the one beneath his father, whose white-stockinged leg he had seen thrust vertically, trembling, into the still air, and the other, who waded peacefully beside his mother. He doesn't ever want to see their faces, he doesn't want to know anything more. The very presence of the thin silver crescent high amid drifts of stars fills him with anxiety and foreboding. Yet he did want to see. He wanted to see.

⇒ BALLOON ⇐

The newly acknowledged leader of the international fireworks avant-garde, Claude Luxo, is leaving his town house. Dressed in evening clothes, and pulling on white gloves, he advances across the vast black-and-white-tiled expanse of the foyer, moving from the great central staircase to the door. Although his face, adorned of late with a sparse moustache, is essentially characterless, if not vapid, on this particular evening, it seems vaguely animated by what might be considered the pleasure of anticipated pleasure; for Luxo is on his way to the theatre to see a performance of *Les Détraquées*. This particular version of the lurid work, presented in English as *The Deranged Ones*, constitutes the first performance of the play in over sixty years.

For reasons much too difficult to discover, let alone assess and judge, Luxo has long loved the play because of one phrase, probably a stage direction: A BALLOON FALLS IN THE ROOM.

He has, certainly, cloudy memories of his impenetrable and indecipherable childhood. On the murky stage of his recollections, his mother most often appears in white shorts, her bleached hair radiant in the sun, her mouth open in nervous laughter as she anxiously embraces a much younger woman, still, almost, a girl. The latter's face is dreamlike, serene, and she wears a white blouse, unbuttoned to the waist, so that her naked breasts are visible when she steps back to look into his mother's eyes. On the edge of this rigidly patterned scene his beautiful young aunt hovers—the appropriate if somewhat fevered word—in a black dress with starched white collar and cuffs, black stockings and pumps; her dark eyes gaze candidly at her sister and the girl, a gaze that is at once subtle, cruel, and despairing.

Luxo has a disturbing, perhaps even wrenching evening in store. So enraptured has he been, all these years, by the imagined spectacle of the play, by the thought of the falling BALLOON, that he has forgotten the essential natures of three of the most important characters: the *principal of the school,* a large blonde of about forty, anxious, nervous, and unable to keep still; the *strange visitor,* a slightly younger, dark and beautiful woman in dark, elegant clothes, black silk stockings, and black heels; and the *young girl,* in a starched and pleated white dress, her face almost imperceptibly corrupted, who walks, tiptoe, across the silence of the stage, directly yet languidly, toward the BALLOON.

There will be revelations: bare thighs, a certain feminine coldness, frantic relatives, a moronic gardener's sinister comments, a black garter, and the bloody corpse of a young girl, at sight of which the audience will gasp and shriek.

Luxo opens the door and walks to his car, nods at the chauffeur, and settles into the luxurious cushions. He smiles, thinking, again, as he has thought, so often, almost all of his life, of that wondrous, suddenly magically apparent BALLOON. It would be interesting to know how he will feel when he arranges and identifies the images of the three actresses, and then begins to make those substitutions which, even now, exist at the border of his consciousness; when he locates himself in both the shabby drama and the unredeemable past.

❧ NOVEL ❧

Mountains, "clothed in gleaming white," as Ström Owns puts it in one of his controversial actualist novels, loomed over the countryside in which stood Olga Chervonen's house. A coincidence, perhaps, yet one no more remarkable than the discovery that Archibald Fuxer appears, in Owns's novel, as Theodore Rosa-Rose, a famous sculptor.

Comments were made, understandably enough, about the mountains, by Mme Chervonen's guests, three samples of which should suffice to represent all: "those are snowy mountains"; "the mountains seem as if clothed in gleaming white"; "the mountains are as if wrapped in snowy mantles." There were also remarks anent a supposedly mysterious snowman and his relationship to the young Archibald Fuxer. They are of little interest.

Fuxer, as art historians are quick to point out, led the way in the movement later known as Mordantism, and some maintain that the most famous of his "white series," called, simply, "White Figures," is a fully achieved Mordantist work, one completed long before the movement was to electrify the art world and change American sculpture forever. In Owns's novel, Rosa-Rose, in a famous scene, is discovered naked and in carnal enjoyment of the snow, his phallus buried "up to its throbbing hilt" in a virgin drift. "Whiteness! Whiteness!" the sculptor gasps. It is a literary moment both enigmatic and serenely dangerous, and following this "powerfully etched image of the artistic temperament," Rosa-Rose discovers that the secrets of form are buried in the *absence of form*. He goes on to fame, wealth, and a gently sad old age, in which he sits surrounded by mementos of the "changeless majesty of the mountains."

To be sure, some well-regarded arbiters of history claim that Archibald Fuxer was no *realer* than Theodore Rosa-Rose, and that the "White Figures" (which, they insist, are attributable to group effort) are a worthless, amateurish clutter of disparate materials, tossed and scrambled together and splattered with white enamel. That Fuxer existed, however, there can be little doubt, for there are records and files, "musty archives in the sad, cavernous basements of old buildings that smelled of despair and failure." And, too, there are many eyewitness accounts of Fuxer, paralyzed with liquor, sprawled in nondescript saloons, "his eyes staring into the abyss of his ruined dreams."

Recent scholarship suggests that the story of the mountains' impact upon art, and especially the art of the mordant, may originally have had to do with Paul Verlaine, whose adventures in the Italian Alps in 1865 are said to have given rise to the poem "Clair de Lune," which appeared in the 1865 volume *Fêtes galantes*. This argument is rooted in the theory that the poem describes three *white figures*, whose evoked presence changes the nature of reality. The figures, *as such*, do not appear in the poem, but students of the period point out that they are quite obviously present as Symbols.

A final note, which may have some bearing on these somewhat arcane matters: lately discovered letters, peripheral to these events, seem to indicate a possible link between Fuxer and Verlaine. Evidence points to startling similarities in their alcoholism, their creative habits, their long descent into wretchedness, their ultimate desuetude, and their uncanny taste in ties. It is information that, surely, "strikes like a hammer blow in the falling snow of a spectral Parisian night!"

⇒ REPETITION ⇐

Carefully dressed in an Oxford grey suit, white shirt, and silver tie of heavy silk, John Cerjet—the very type of the successful bank officer—half-turned away from his study desk, raised an 8 millimeter Raymond automatic to his head, and shot himself through the right temple. Centered on his desk blotter was a letter addressed to his lawyer. It read, in its entirety:

I am ending my life because I can no longer find any joy in it. My wife is dead, my children are distant, and my old friends seem like strangers to me. I have just looked over my will, and it is, in all particulars, satisfactory.

John Cerjet

Why it should have been that Cerjet could "no longer find any joy in" his life cannot be discovered, although there were as many theories as there were gossips and snoops to broadcast them. Unknown to these anxious information addicts, however, was a file, but lately acknowledged as important, containing unsorted psychoanalytic notes on what was darkly called the "lake man" case. The patient was identical, in all particulars, to Cerjet, although his name appears nowhere in the file. It is possible, with a judicious guess here and a reasonable conjecture there, to piece together the essential structure of the case, which rested on a regularly recurring dream, one that, at one point in the patient's life, was repeated every night for the better part of six months.

In the dream, three young women of about seventeen are in the bedroom of a comfortable house on a quiet country road. They are dressing for Mass, and, then, are identically beautiful in gauzy white summer dresses with snug bodices, high collars, and full skirts. They wear white stockings and shoes, and on their heads balance Missals which are white lace-trimmed handkerchiefs pinned to their hair. On the way to church, amid a great deal of laughter and blushes, they abruptly find themselves off the road, amid tall grass which is the clear shallows of a lake in whose cool waters they wade, sheltered from the sun by enormous shade trees. They hold their skirts immodestly high, so high that their surprising nakedness is wantonly exposed. Behind a tree, a man, partially hidden in deep shadows, and with an arbalest strapped to his back, stares at them in horror as he masturbates.

The dreamer, who can see into the man's mind, who is, absolutely, the man's thoughts, knows that the man knows that he is watching his mother as a young woman, that *each* of the young women, in some obscure parody or mockery of the Holy Trinity, is his mother. But he is helpless in this knowledge, and in an agony of shame, continues to surrender himself to his vile pleasure. The dreamer, aware of what is going to happen, tries desperately to dream the young women away from the lake, dream them into oblivion, for he knows that they will discover the man hidden in the shadows, and so they do. Now, just before the dreamer wakes, the young women, in precisely choreographed synchronicity, turn to face the man so as lewdly to display themselves, naked, to him. Their eyes widen in shocked recognition as he ejaculates, groaning, and they open their mouths to scream, or laugh, or, perhaps, to cry out lasciviously.

The dream apparently became insupportable to Cerjet, and its merciless pattern of repetition may have exhausted his spirit. It is probably going too far to say that the dream was the direct cause of his suicide, although it was, clearly, symptomatic of some profound disturbance. One puzzling comment, scribbled on a fragment of note paper found in the file, reads:

lake man aware may be man in shads but such knldg no help

⇒ LOZENGE ⇐

Here is the partial text of a letter from Jenny Hounsfield to Bill Juillard. The asterisks indicate lacunae in the original:

Dear Bill,

I shouldn't ask you what I know will get a negative reply. I know that there is only one woman for you, even though that woman is only a dream, or a memory, which is the same thing. She hardly exists and yet there she is and always will be, although I *** hopes. Always! But I'm so miserable, Bill dear, that if you could only come for a little while my spirits would be really lifted. Ivan will be away on business next week for 10 days, so ***

That was really the finish of it for me and killed whatever love I might have had left for him. And I've told you how much I did love *** beginning. But there is no other word for what he did but rape, pure and simple. I felt so filthy and soiled that I threw away the skirt and slip I was wearing *** his terrible cartoons all the time, or whatever he calls them and gets strange and frightening. I won't even try to tell you *** dinner party *** some disgusting Dean of something rubbing up against me all night in his fatherly way, and Ivan was *** the while.

*** know it's crazy, sometimes I stand at the window with hardly any clothes on *** from the waist up, hoping that somebody will see me and want me and take me *** man! *** insane, I think, with his ideas about blood purification and vegetable enemas and nutshells *** laughing *** he's given up wearing underwear because of what he says is seminal-corpuscle death or something that *** the neighborhood thinks I'm a tramp and feels sorry for poor Ivan, I have to ***

As I also may have written, there isn't a day passes that I'm not sore or black and blue and my breasts covered with bruises and bites. The other day I looked *** cried at the way ***

Can't you come next week, dear, dear Bill? I can't forget our meetings and there was nothing sordid about them, not to me, and *** parked cars and bathrooms nor that the first time you were soaked, as you said, in gin. I thought ***

I don't especially like to carry secrets around either but if I must I must. Please, Bill, 10 days for the two ***

all love,
Jenny

Bill Juillard looked at the date on the letter, written thirty-five years earlier, almost to the day. He sat quietly on the edge of "the Void," a wishing well, that, popularly, had no bottom, and which was sought out by lovers desirous of calling down maledictions on the heads of those who would stymie their love.

Bill was in a white linen suit, a blue-and-white repp-striped tie, and a Panama hat. He carried a thin Malacca cane. He thought of Jenny and her disastrous life, which it had, perhaps, been in his power to ameliorate, or even change permanently. But he had been inhabited, and was, still, by the neurotic and paralyzing memory of the girl whose *essence*, somehow, had become one with a tree. Without fail, he had helplessly followed the path of the tree. Through miseries, elations, triumphs, failures, and obsessions, he had followed the path of the tree. Yet at the edges of his mind there had always been the blissful actuality of Jenny's desirous body.

He shook his head and folded the letter into a very small lozenge, then dropped it into "the Void." It was time to start home. But out of the corner of his eye, he saw a flash of white. The letter had risen up through the cold gloom of the well, and now hovered at the level of Juillard's eyes. It was like nothing so much as a tiny white balloon, floating, miraculously suspended, bitterly recriminatory.

⮞ HAT ⮜

Much to the surprise of the staff at Sunset Haven, Jonathan Tancred, since his transfer from Pelepzin, had been the pro-verbial model patient—calm, cooperative, and responsive to treatment. All the more strange then that, against regulations, he took to wearing a hat, one crudely fashioned from a pillow-case: It was an odd-looking affair, in shape something between a beret and a chef's toque. He refused to remove it, and the attendants, under inflexible orders, immediately carried the news of this breach of hospital rules to the administration.

Tancred was called before the senior staff committee the next day so as to explain his reasons for flouting regulations. Without hesitation, he began by saying that his nervous system had been turned into a network of wires along which Dr. Lelgach, *supposedly* his attending psychiatrist at Pelepzin, sends depraved and perverted messages to his brain in her attempt to corrupt him with lust so as to force him to give up his solitary crusade to destroy all the *evidence* and *official memories* that threaten Christian America and the concept of a relevant Jesus. The messages, he told the committee, began at his first interview with her. When she crossed her legs he felt the first terrible influence of the "words-not-mine" that she controlled; her messages ran wild and electric along his wire-nerves and directly into his brain.

He leaned forward and looked from one committee member to another, then, lowering his voice, said that there was some-thing, some sort of device hidden under her skirt that generated the messages, some awful machine between her legs. But his hat now prevented the messages from reaching his brain, and although his wire-nerves seemed to blaze with fire when the messages were thwarted, this agony was preferable to the abnormally filthy commands and ideas and suggestions sent by Dr. Lelgach.

The hat, Tancred continued, also, he knew, permitted him to discover, just yesterday, that Dr. Lelgach was attempting to send messages to the president of the United States! Lewd and debased and lascivious descriptions and unnatural injunctions intended to make him and all our Christian leaders and then all Americans everywhere fall under the command of demonic powers, deny Jesus, and squander pure-blooded energy fornicating uninterruptedly with mongrel races and doing corrupt and unspeakable things to highly moral and clean-living men and women, just like pigs and Arabs and Jew atheists. They and their slaves and dupes are the ones who want to preserve the EVIDENCE and the OFFICIAL MEMORIES in places like the schoolbooks that teach about putting out the cleansing fires with homosexuals in charge of the fire departments everywhere!

He leaned back in his chair. He had a theory that Dr. Lelgach was really a trained Communist prostitute who sexually bribed her way into the Pelepzin Hospital in order to pose as a psychiatrist so as to be assigned to his case, because he knew full well that the demonic Jew-Arabs were aware of his lonely fight. Her perfume, for instance, at their first interview, gave him a terrible headache and aroused him to the point at which he was forced to stare at the doctor's legs and even brazenly try to see up her skirt, which was much too short, while she, like the degenerate whore she was, *pretended* to pull her skirt down and keep her thighs closed, but it was a farce, of course, for it was then, when she seemed most modest, that she let him see, as if by accident, the machine, flickering with blue sparks, that she had planted between her legs! She told him, as he helplessly stared at it, that although it looked like nothing more than a little box, it was really an automatic gnomon, designed to recall lost memories, so, of course, he realized that she had also arranged for the gnomon on the garden wall to be installed. He should have known!

He hadn't been fooled, though, by her false purity and confidences, for he knew that although she exposed herself, she was actually guarding the loathsome evidence, as well as sending "words-not-mine" messages along his wire-nerves. He later wrote her a note telling her that he had discovered some of the evidence that she was hiding underneath her doctor *costume*, because he had been able, with the help of prayers to Jesus and meditations on the president of the United States and his wonderful close-knit family, to see through her whore clothes, thank God! And to see what he *wanted* to see, not the hideous sex-organ-machine box that she wanted him to stare at until he felt very disturbed. At this point, he was summarily transferred to Sunset Haven. He knew that the doctors here wanted to study him and he would continue to be very cooperative. But he had to have his hat or Dr. Lelgach's messages would destroy his mind forever.

Wasn't there anything, he wondered, that the psychiatric profession, or the district attorney, or the CIA could do about this doctor prostitute? Couldn't some undercover agent watch her undress one day with a special infrared telescope, or maybe she could be forced to strip her clothes off before a panel of Christian experts? Then they could disconnect the destructive machine between her legs and have it analyzed at the FBI laboratories to pinpoint the source of its hellish powers. And shouldn't the president of the United States be warned that the unspeakable thoughts he has probably been entertaining are not really his?

Tancred by now had grown extremely agitated and his voice had risen to a high, keening whine. One of the committee members nodded almost imperceptibly to the attendants, alert behind the patient's chair, and they moved forward quietly. "My hat, my hat," Tancred sobbed, placing both hands over his head and the hat crammed down upon it. "I need my hat."

⇒ FRUITS ⇐

When Mr. Chainville wakes, often still clad in his navy-blue melton overcoat and grey snap-brim fedora, he doesn't know whether he is Mr. Chainville, who has just dreamt of Gregory Balbet, or Gregory Balbet, who has imagined Mr. Chainville for the express purpose of forcing Mr. Chainville to dream of Gregory Balbet. This is a common experience among dreamers and those with finely tuned imaginations. Gregory Balbet is the international pistol champion, often called, by his admirers, "a crack shot," "a great shot," and "a wonderful shot." They are not given to fustian.

It is generally accepted, though not proven, that Mr. Chainville has not been imagined by Gregory Balbet, but that he is Donald Chainville's father, and the president of Three Maids Home Products, Inc., manufacturers of, among other things, laundry hampers of a surpassing ugliness. He is on the edge of bankruptcy, which is, perhaps, why he dreams of Gregory Balbet, who is dressed, in perfect dreamwork fashion, in a navy-blue melton overcoat and a grey snap-brim fedora. Balbet, with what his aforementioned admirers call "a studied nonchalance," "an elegant insouciance," and "an aristocratic panache," is aiming his favorite pistol, a 10.3 millimeter Vitalium revolver of glistening blue steel, directly at Emilia Bex *née* Sladky, who, in the usual manner of female jugglers, stands provocatively costumed, at center stage, the air about her filled with flying fruit and other objects too banal to record, at least for everyone but Dr. Lelgach, for whom "this subtle affair," as she puts it, is a clinical case "fraught with drama," another of her phrases. It is understood that the flying fruit and other objects—all sped into graceful parabolas by Mrs. Bex's clever hands—are sometimes regarded as symbols. "But of *what!*" Dr. Lelgach asks. "It is the *name* of the fruit, etc., etc., which matters, and not the fruit, etc., etc., itself." As she speaks, she compulsively pulls her skirt down over her knees, or perhaps she pulls the name "skirt" down over the word "knees." In any event, she seems slightly feverish.

When Mr. Chainville wakes, often still clad in his street clothes, some articles of which are by now quite familiar, he wonders who Dr. Lelgach can be. He also wonders why Balbet never fires at the female juggler, or, as Chainville has been taught to say, juggleress.

This dream, or whatever, and others much like it, but for minor variants, continued for some time, always occurring in the present, or what Mr. Chainville thought of as the present. It was *his* present, anyway, so the dream was ever fresh, if, he wondered, "fresh" is a word.

Mrs. Bex, or so Dr. Lelgach insists, juggled, on most days, an apple, an orange, a banana, a hatchet, a toy zeppelin, and a doorknob leased by the month from a dirty joke; and on other days, different fruits and certain other etceteras. Significantly, other contemporary investigators, greatly assisted by notes and letters in the possession of Mr. Chainville's son, Donald, are in rare agreement in their opinion that Gregory Balbet became a pistol champion *after* he first saw Mrs. Bex perform. Which, quite probably, means precisely that which it so obviously, yet incredibly, signifies. These things considered, it is puzzling that Dr. Lelgach has become bogged down in her study, which now looks as if it might never be completed. Yanking furiously at her skirt, she shakes her head in disagreement, and lights the filter end of a cigarette. She seems depressed.

Mr. Chainville wakes, dressed in his navy-blue melton overcoat and grey snap-brim fedora. He has no idea why he is behind the wheel of his Packard, parked beneath a mammoth tree.

≫ BENCH ≪

It was on this lovingly preserved bench that Robert Bedu proposed to his future wife, Claudia, who, upon the occasion, assented vaguely, her eyes, shaded by her enormous straw picture hat, languidly gazing into the deep shadows of the foliage surrounding. The bench was, too, the original site for the preparation of Bedu's notorious Greek salads, much loved by Dr. Ronald LeFlave. Surrounded by the myriad ingredients needed to make—"construct," was the sometime chef's word—the perfect salad, Bedu had invariably worn a white linen suit, white shoes, and a white Borsalino, an affectation of dress which endeared him to many of the inhabitants of the Compound, but which struck others, perhaps of more discriminating taste, as the certain vulgarity of a provincial fop. Bedu, with the placid equanimity of a long-popular inventor, paid neither admirers nor detractors any heed, but persisted, as usual and as scheduled, with his familiar culinary project.

Some of the spectral trees amid which the bench stands seemed, during that era, to be laden with snow, which, on closer inspection, proved to be white paint. This may account for the fact that the cheery snowman, to which Dr. LeFlave had prepared himself to become accustomed, was conspicuously absent. The planned Winter Wonderland tableau was, of course, hopelessly compromised, to say the least.

Bedu's assistants, three young women attractively clad in filmy summer dresses, almost always aided him in the preparation of the salad—one chopping olives, another tearing lettuce, a third measuring oil, and so on—although there were times when they simply posed, arms linked, against the weird trees. Having decided on the latter action, they'd identify themselves, with much laughter and blushing, by means of placards hung around their necks. One read GIRL IN THE CELLAR; another, DROWNED LONA; and a third, WOMAN AT THE WINDOW. It is quite clear that they were ignorant of the import of these uncanny signs.

Although the young women made a great show of being good sports, as drowned Lona put it, they were bitterly disappointed by the lack of the simplest amenities, amenities which Bedu had sworn to provide. So it was that in order to wash their hands and cool their faces and necks, it was necessary for them to plunge through heavy thickets and marshy ground to reach the banks of a dark, still lake. Once there, although the cold water was inviting, they considered it an offense to modesty to remove their slippers and stockings and, skirts held about their thighs, slowly wade in the shallows, for they knew that Dr. LeFlave, hidden among the trees, would be watching. The same fear of the doctor's voyeurism prevented them from relieving themselves in the brush, and they often performed their work in acute discomfort.

Perhaps most humiliating was their knowledge that they were under constant observation by Mrs. Bedu, who had, and more than once, called them little whores. The young women, virgins, of course, would redden in shame and indignation. That Mrs. Bedu regularly followed Dr. LeFlave—whom she called "Rondee"—to a small canvas lean-to he'd thrown up amid giant ferns, made her attacks on them seem all the more intolerably hypocritical. The girl in the cellar's diary speaks of this time as one in which the trio yearned for nothing more than a spotless kitchen. This desperate remark has made them the target of much contemporary feminist criticism. The bronze memorial plaque on the bench quite properly tells the visitor nothing of all this: the Compound had its rules and traditions, despite shifting ideologies.

That all we know of these events derives from a series of photographs does not preclude the reality of Bedu's Greek salads and the phenomena attendant upon their construction, even if, as recent research has rather convincingly argued, the photographs are of scenes from the Blue Bird Regional Theatre's production of a forgotten melodrama, *The Salad Bench*.

⧽ ZEPPELIN ⧼

A pronounced thrill of excitement in the airless, ill-humored world of Neo-Gravis poetry has been occasioned by the recent discovery—attributed to Norman Bob, the sensational new performance artist—of what is said to be another photograph of Leonard Bacon. Curiously, it seems to have been taken during the same Zo Mountains hiking trip that gave the literary world the adored and classic likeness of the supreme craftsman.

There are some difficulties surrounding the newly found photograph, which shows Bacon standing on the flimsy catwalk that girdles Mt. Banjo some nine hundred feet below its rugged peak. He leans on a walking stick, his head bent slightly forward, his right hand cupped behind his right ear in an attitude of attentive listening. But, as said, there *are* some difficulties, beginning with the walking stick that is here substituted for the staff in the classic image; and although Bacon's cap, breeches, and sweater seem identical in both photographs, as does his nonchalantly borne puta bag, the poet is not wearing his wonted dashing boots, but is in unprepossessing puttees and cumbersome hiking shoes.

Most troubling, however, to those who, like Benno DeLux, consider themselves to have been especially close to the poet is the aspect of Bacon's head, which he carries in such fashion that its forward tilt, in combination with the pulled-down bill of his cap, serves partially to obscure the subject's features. Once again, the question of identity arises to drain some of what *Atelier Verse Review* termed "triumphant sweetness" from the discovery; on the other hand, all but the most cynical have agreed, gingerly, to accept the photograph, provisionally, at least, as an authentic image of the worshiped author.

Lively discussions have arisen concerning Bacon's listening attitude, virtually all of them focused on the question of just *what* he was listening to, or for. The prose-disabled suggest, unanimously, that he was hearkening to nature herself, or to those things that may be held "natural in themselves," as they phrase it, e.g., mountain zephyrs, echoes of the avalanche, a soughing of dying trees, the cries of sward hawks, and the slow tread of the secretive leech-gatherers. Others feel that Bacon was, logically speaking, alert to the possibly anguished sounds made by the partially clad woman he so poetically espied. Still others argue that he was listening, ravished, to the musical offerings of Helga, the hermit ghost, who, so the tales have it, stumbled to her death, mad with forbidden love for her "Mr. Ferret," from a catwalk much like that seen in the photograph.

Perhaps the most arresting theory, if such a word may be applied to what even an *elementary* hermeneutics of hidden ontologies considers nothing but a crackpot idea, is the view held by Professor Joshua Bex. He maintains that Bacon's attitude is clearly that of a man who hears the distant engines of a zeppelin. Unexpectedly elegant though wholly unprovable, this theory has gained popularity among those who favor deeper meanings and gender stances in contemporary verse, insofar as these programmatics may be calibrated with market demands. Others merely laugh and point to the well-known supposition that the suffocating velvets and bibelots of the sort amid which Bex lived for years wreak irreversible havoc on the brain. To such charges, Professor Bex, on the "Pegasus Hour" radio program, smilingly remarked, "The zeppelin characteristically displays the word BALLOON on either side of its—I wish to emphasize this—*phallic* shape!"

The station, as might be guessed, was flooded with phone calls, many delivered in perfect iambics, nature's measure.

≫ IMAGES ≪

It was recently discovered that the book containing the slightly blurred and hypnotic passage filled with silence, sought for by Donald Chainville more than forty years, is not a book at all, but a film. Chainville, it appears, in his brooding, substituted words for the original cinematic images, allowing the words to create, as they invariably will, their own images, new images that drove out the old, so as to become the truth. Over the years, decreasingly patient friends as well as worried professional associates hesitantly suggested the possibility that the images to which Chainville returned, again and again, were "too good to be true," in this instance a remarkably apt expression. They were, in short, sick of the navy-blue melton overcoat, grey snap-brim fedora, bitter-cold skies and pale sunset, Packard sedan, etc., etc. Some even questioned Chainville's sanity, and to his face. To such thankfully rare impertinence, he would reply, "But why then does the boy run away?" They were difficult years.

To this day, Chainville still regularly searches for the nonexistent passage in the nonexistent book, but without the fevered diligence displayed in his young manhood. Interestingly enough, there is a scene in the film that occurs directly following the flight scene, one that adds another element of mystery to the story. The man is seen from behind, ringing the doorbell of what the viewer knows is the boy's house. He has changed into a frock coat and a tall silk hat and he carries a black cane. From inside the house we can hear a woman's voice, a distant and hollow-sounding whisper: it is intimate, provocative, even, improbably, tempting, although its timbre belies the message that it carries.

"You can't see him, and you and the bitch together can't certainly see him either. I want you to die and the bitch with you! Just send the money, all *right?*, just send the money!"

Undisturbed, the man continues to ring the bell. Its soft

chimes can be heard within, through the closed door.

"*See* him?" the man says in a conversational tone. "I don't want to *see* him! I want my Packard model, my snow photographs, my Worcestershire sauce, and my neatly tied bundle of intimate personal correspondence, mostly sexual. Speaking of which, didn't my little whore of a secretary look wonderful in the tight white dress that she wore to your birthday party? Or was that his birthday party? Underneath she was naked, of course. We fucked standing up in the pantry later. Nice?"

"I'm at the sink in the dim kitchen," the woman's voice replies, hoarse with an almost burlesque sensuality.

"Believe me, I don't give a good God damn about Donald. He's *your* son. *See* him! Jesus, that's a good one!" The man laughs. "And oh yes, I also need my navy-blue melton overcoat now that the winter's coming."

"Come on in, I'm not decent," the woman's voice offers.

The man continues to ring the bell as the scene slowly fades out.

It is probably for the best that Chainville never remembered this film, the source of the falsified imagery with which he could live. This doorstep scene would have certainly made him powerless to metamorphose and relocate its images, to turn its callous dialogue into metaphor: to soften it, that is, into bittersweet sadness.

⇒ CHANT ⇐

Dr. Lelgach looked out the window, unnerved, despite her experience, by the laughing maniacs scattered about the grounds in varied displays of uncontrolled movement. Some of the lunatics jerked here and there, arm in arm, others fell to their knees repeatedly, and a few thrashed about on the ground in antic choreographies. Especially disturbing were the three women in newspaper hats clustered just beneath her window; they grinned and shouted and made strangely ingenuous lewd gestures. Perhaps she had, indeed, been doing this too long, much too long. She turned to the desk and the letter she had carefully postponed reading. Lifting it to her nose, she smelled Stephen Alcott's cologne, heard his voice, saw his troubled eyes. This last phrase struck her as somewhat melodramatic.

The dark hallway on that second night. The other guests in dead sleep. The recognition! Soon after, the conversation with her fiancé—difficult, stupid, cruel, wounding. He was shocked and bitterly incredulous. Stephen Alcott? A hack writer? Stephen *Alcott?* No help for it. Cruel and difficult. She fingered the rich linen paper of the envelope, annoyed at the lack of a return address. What was he afraid of? He had often spoken of his late wife, Isabella, and of how he had hated the fact that their house was only *hers*, just as his mother's house had been only *hers.* The blissfully dead past, he would say when she asked him about the dark lacustrine picture he'd taken from his mother's living room after her death. Perhaps that was the name of the painting.

She slit the envelope open and pulled the letter out, her fingers aware of the engraved Gothic "A" which they touched. She wanted a letter filled with longing and passion, overt in its erotic imaginings and desires, a candid letter, a lover's letter. Not his usual sober and respectful and vaguely humble periods. A *lover's* letter! The screams from the Recreation Circle seemed remarkably loud, quite out of the ordinary. She smoothed the sheet of stationery out on her desk and put on her glasses.

Madness, rage, and
Frantic fury

Place and situate
The Laws and Rites

That, ashen grey, are
Speckled like a starling.

Do you like this poem, Doc.? It's my considered comment on the filthy EVIDENCE I have on you. Of course you know I can see right through your doctor costume and right through you too! Your electric box doesn't bother me anymore, you perverted bitch.

Dr. Lelgach read the letter again, as if compelled. There was a terrible din at the window, louder than before, and, again, as if compelled, she looked out. The three women, waving their hats in the air, were chanting, quite clearly, in unison: MANÉ THESEL PSARES! MANÉ THESEL PSARES! MANÉ THESEL PSARES! Dr. Lelgach had no idea what these sounds meant, but they chilled her, and she swallowed against a growing nausea. She began to straighten her cluttered desk, occasionally interrupting this task to smooth, nervously, her skirt over her thighs and down her legs to its hem. Then she abruptly vomited.

⊰ THINGS ⊱

If it was possible, on the spur of the moment, to gather together enough people for a vaguely ridiculous and somewhat unconventional memorial service for a man whom almost everyone despised, then it was perhaps inevitable that such evidence of decadence would, soon after, drive an inspired psychopath to set a devastating warehouse fire, one destined to become yet another famous disaster fixed in group memory. In some curious and unexplained manner, a demented-looking *snowman* was caught up in these events: a partly clothed woman, from her vantage in the shadows of a dim kitchen, has testified to his brooding presence.

His design—if a snowman can be said to have a design—was elaborated by a creative team in one of the old houses on the cobblestoned street that flaunts several newly installed antique gas lamps, designed to please well-heeled if gauche visitors. They are enchanted by the Old House, an old house whose candid whiteness is that of new snow, and by the wonderful, although temporary, absence of all sound. They admire, as well, the picture postcards, available almost anywhere, of famous views, although the series depicting gloomy equestriennes is out of print. Still, the "Venerable Trees" series is available, and as popular as ever.

The carefully yellowed photograph of the poetically garbed mountain climber has fallen into disrepute, since the man has lately been confused in the popular mind with the disreputable voyeur charged with spying on three sisters and their brother at youthful play beneath the moon. The pervert blustered that he had merely been following the movements of jaunty fox-hunters so as to record their loud reactions to a female scare-crow which he himself had erected, so to speak, in a stubble field.

This story, ridiculous on its face, became even shakier when witnesses claimed that the accused degenerate was often recognized at Mass, dressed in women's clothes. A young wife corroborated this testimony, and a bank statement in her possession was inexplicably placed into evidence. So time passed, "country shadows," as the poem says, "fell dark across the sundial," and rude craftsmen smiled contentedly at the very simplicity of divers barnyard joys.

In the city, bitter litigation concerning badly cut velvet proceeded apace, vandalized fountains plashed in the littered squares, and moth-eaten jugglers entertained hostile crowds outside the Moon Adventure exhibition, with its breathtaking although spurious vistas of that lunar meadow known as *Terra Incognita* (or, *The Beach*).

The rich, as always, exchanged vapid calling cards and brandished sticks and parasols, jostling each other for the most prominent seats at the muted-violin recitals they barely suffered. Discreet naps furnished them with dreams of capital gains and mounds of massive, robust sandwiches, amid which nobly born figures in white glared stupidly. One of the newer, more revolting casinos, where almost anything crudely French might happen, was, alas, part of the gay evening rounds.

Mornings after, so to speak, more often than not found many of the more obstreperous gentlemen carrying injured arms in slings, while certain wives, fiancées, and pals displayed early symptoms of loathsome diseases. It was certain that small cafés that specialized in dominoes, loneliness, and casually placed bowls filled with luminous balls did frantic business; and those establishments that offered bouts of supper theatre were even more crowded, especially when plays dealing with military themes were staged: the razzle-dazzle "theatre of velleity" offering, *Key Passages*, a series of fifty-nine waywardly abstruse blackouts, was the hit of the season.

Quieter citizens sequestered themselves in the country, amid barren fields, scabby farmyard beasts, and wintry sunsets, delighted to be away from their desks and the overpowering desire, even the need, to doze fitfully while presumably hard at work. Social obligations required that they suffer an occasional trip into the city on the old endearing rattletrap of a train, and the conductors, in such circumstance, seemed especially repulsive. The drunkenly ascending balloon or two, glimpsed through sooty windows, depressed the travelers' spirits even further!

Because the world moved so predictably, so blindly, it came as no surprise that beautiful young mothers were everywhere found, breasts bared, tears running uncontrollably down their faces; nor was it startling to come across, on street corners, wildly dancing lunatics. A great artist sat, forgotten and paralyzed with liquor, in a filthy saloon, and a celebrated chemist finished writing an intimate letter whose most important particulars were consciously distorted, when not absolutely false.

Lonely people cringed and smiled grotesquely at their supplicant reflections in mirrors, then asked anguished questions of the silent darkness. Sometimes, to guard themselves from despair and the black pit of masturbation, they attended public meetings of furious tenants' councils or self-righteous neighborhood action committees, or even subjected themselves to the crude insults of vulgar waiters in expensive restaurants, momentarily content to be fools among fools.

There was, not unexpectedly, a great deal of money counted and stacked and stolen and counted and stacked and stolen again. There was, for the leisured, the exquisite pleasure of writing inane notes on rich, creamy stationery. There was the sudden message, obscure yet terrifying, screeched out by the mangy parrot in the street. And, without fail, there were countless obsolete foundation garments, crazed horses, adult-education courses, and secret perversions of a religious nature.

It was no wonder, then, that it seemed to sensitive and alert men and women that language had begun to collapse and then dissolve, so that even the simplest banking transactions became excruciating episodes in suffocating pretentiousness, based on false systems of hierarchy and constantly eroding signifiers.

There were stories, all too common, of wildly staring diners, their faces pallid, suddenly swallowing the contents of bottles filled with poison; and for one man, a snatch of Aeolic verse brought to mind long-forgotten, intolerable chapters from his life to fill him with horror.

On the fringes of these private as well as civic manifestations of futility, small theatre companies found it profitable to present fabulously lurid plays from earlier eras, and alarmingly inept novels, known as "instant classics" to newspaper drudges, sold by the millions to the highly literate. A respected banker shot himself to death because of his unfashionable dreams, and, for one elegant gentleman, a sudden suspension of the laws of nature turned his hair as white as his summery suit.

The mental hospitals, sanitariums, lunatic asylums, and prisons were crammed with sincere maniacs, all of whom had a staggeringly sophisticated command of psycho-sociological jargon. An international pistol champion took aim at what he said he most loved—*flying fruit.* One of the world's most revered inventors began his third year as an open-air constructor of Greek salads, and the mountains, just a quick eighteen hours away on the turnpike, were said to echo continuously with threatening messages.

Importunate visitors to the archives were mockingly informed by the aesthetic authorities that the truth could—*perhaps*—be found in a certain unnamed film, but was absent from all texts. As if to strengthen the validity of this coarse opinion, the revered Greek quotation above the entrance to the municipal courts building was found to be not Greek at all, but non-sensical ciphers. The stars, in their trillions, shone on these people and phenomena, on these credos, tears, and *things,* on this vast desire, shone and shone, meaningless.

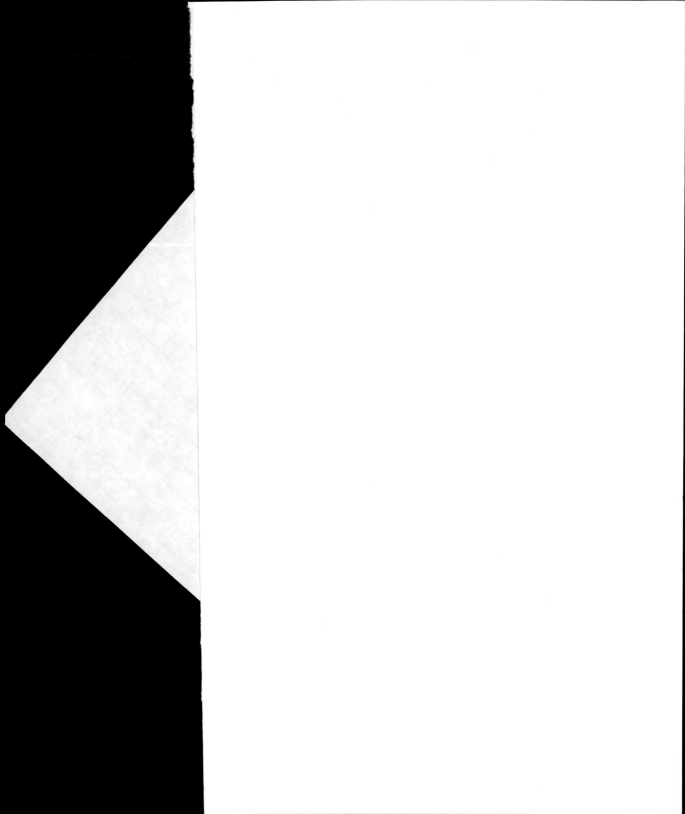

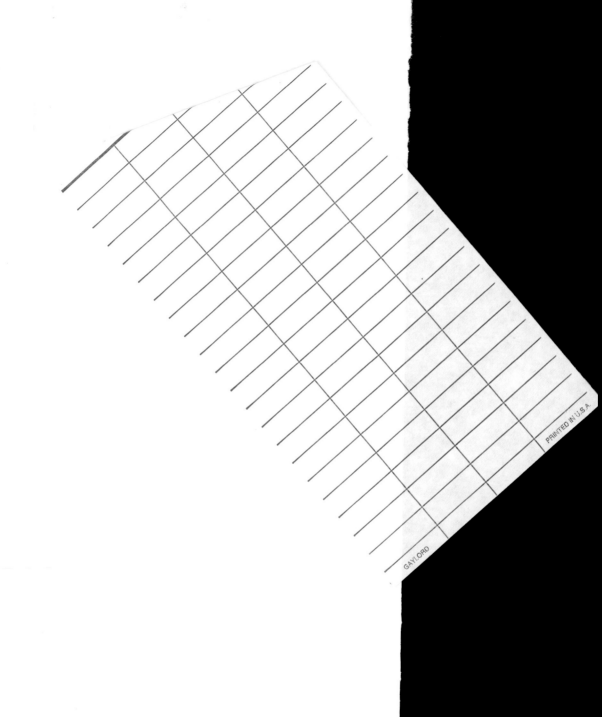

GAYLORD

PRINTED IN U.S.A.